FIVE STAR ATTRACTION

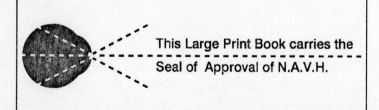

This Large Print Book carries the
Seal of Approval of N.A.V.H.

FIVE STAR ATTRACTION

JACQUELIN THOMAS

THORNDIKE PRESS

A part of Gale, Cengage Learning

GALE
CENGAGE Learning·

Detroit • New York • San Francisco • New Haven, Conn • Waterville, Maine • London

LIBRARY OF CONGRESS CATALOGING-IN-PUBLICATION DATA

Thomas, Jacquelin.
    Five star attraction / by Jacquelin Thomas. — Large print ed.
      p. cm. — (Thorndike Press large print African-American)
    ISBN 978-1-4104-4470-7 (hardcover) — ISBN 1-4104-4470-8 (hardcover)
    1. African Americans—Fiction. 2. Widowers—Fiction. 3. Consultants—Fiction. 4. Large type books. I. Title.
    PS3570.H5637F58 2012
    813'.54—dc23   2012004389

Published in 2012 by arrangement with Harlequin Books S.A.

Printed in Mexico
1 2 3 4 5 6 7 16 15 14 13 12

This book is dedicated to my wonderful husband who also happens to be my best friend. I look forward to waking up and spending each day with you. Thank you for 20 fabulous years!

Dear Reader,

What would you do if you suddenly found that you were the heir to a vast fortune? In the first book of my new series introducing the Alexanders of Beverly Hills, you will meet a wonderful new family who find themselves in the midst of a real-life rags-to-riches story. I have always been a fan of the Beverly Hillbillies, so I must confess that they actually inspired my new series. I'm very excited about introducing Malcolm, his wife, Barbara, and their six children to you.

In *Five Star Attraction,* you will get to know Malcolm's oldest son, Ari, a widower who works nonstop to keep from dwelling on his singleness until he meets Natasha LeBlanc, a smart and sexy business consultant hired to help his family manage the luxury chain of hotel and spa resorts. I hope you will enjoy their journey to happily ever after. Thanks for your support and don't forget to email me at jacquelinthomas@yahoo .com. I'd love to hear from you!

Sincerely,
Jacquelin

CHAPTER 1

"Dad, what are you thinking about?" Ari Alexander asked.

His father sat with his brows drawn together in an agonized expression. He hadn't said much since learning he was the only heir to the late Robert DePaul's vast estate, which included the chain of luxury DePaul Hotel & Spa Resorts.

Three days ago, they were just a family living a normal life in the small town of Aspen, Georgia, located forty miles west of Atlanta. They had been thrust into the limelight with the news that Malcolm Alexander was the illegitimate love child between the hotel magnate and Pearle Strickland, an African American woman.

"Dad," Ari prompted. "You okay?"

"Just wondering why my mother never thought she could tell me about him," Malcolm replied. "She never once mentioned Robert DePaul. I have no idea how she could've met him. As far as I know, she never left Georgia. She did tell me that Theodore Alexander wasn't my biological father, but that never mattered to me. He was a good father."

He drew his lips in thoughtfully then glanced out the window of the private plane transporting them to Los Angeles. "She never volunteered any other information about my real father, and I never asked her about him, but now I wish I had. Knowing about Robert DePaul could've prepared me some for all this." He shrugged. "My mind is going in a hundred different directions."

Ari nodded in understanding. Robert DePaul had been one of the richest men in the world until his death a week ago. His attorney contacted Ari's father, and now they were headed to meet with Ira Goodman.

"I keep wondering where Grandma met DePaul."

Malcolm gave a slight shrug. "Son, I suppose we won't ever find out, but evidently their paths must have crossed at some point, if what they're saying is true."

"The media are having a field day with this," Ari uttered. "Robert DePaul's African-American son is sole heir to his fortune. I can't wait to see the expression on the faces of our newfound relatives. I can read the headlines now — 'The Georgia Hillbillies Are Moving to Beverly Hills.' "

"Our family lives just fine, Ari," Malcolm interjected quickly. "We don't have to take this man's money or anything he owns. I'm only flying out there to learn more about the man who fathered me — not committing to anything else."

A muscle quivered at Ari's jaw. "Dad, he was your father, and legally, you *are* entitled to everything DePaul left in his will for you. It's your legacy."

"Just because I'm entitled doesn't mean I want it," Malcolm responded. He rested his chin on his hand.

Ari gave Malcolm a sidelong glance. "What does Mom think about all this?"

"You know your mother," Malcolm said. His mouth curved into an unconscious smile. "She told me that she's fine with whatever I decide to do."

That sounded exactly like his mother, Ari thought. Barbara Alexander trusted her husband's instincts as much as she relied on her own. His parents were partners in business as well as in life, and perfect examples of what a good marriage should look like.

Ari glanced down at the wedding band on

11

his left ring finger, his heart saturated with grief.

At thirty-two years old, Ari was a widower, having lost his wife to cancer. He was still dealing with her death two years later.

He glanced over at his father, who appeared to be deep in thought. Ari and his siblings all agreed that their father should accept his inheritance, but they knew that their deeply spiritual parents would not make a decision until they spent time in prayer, seeking divine guidance.

Ari couldn't understand why his father would willingly walk away from his inheritance. His parents and grandparents had worked in the hospitality industry for as long as Ari could remember, and they often talked about owning a chain of high-end hotels. This was a dream come true — not just for his mom and dad, but also for him.

They owned two hotels that were performing well, but they always dreamed of expanding. Ari loved working alongside his parents, and this once-in-a-lifetime opportunity to manage a conglomerate like the DePaul Hotel Group was just too tempting to pass up.

Ultimately, it was his father's decision, and his alone to make. Despite what Ari felt about it, he would respect Malcolm's choice.

The May temperature in California was what Ari considered comfortable. It wasn't extremely hot and it wasn't as humid as it was back home.

They had arrived at the Los Angeles International Airport fifteen minutes ago and were now in a sleek, black limousine on the way to Beverly Hills. Ari and his family had traveled to California for vacation once, but it had been years ago. Nothing looked familiar except for the palm trees and all of the nonstop traffic that flowed around them.

In Aspen, there were no hour-long commutes to work in a sea of heavy traffic, no outrageously priced real estate markets, no driving all the way across town to reach his favorite stores or restaurants.

In Aspen, the residents knew one another. Los Angeles would take some getting used to, Ari decided. The only time he'd left Aspen for a length of time was when he attended college in Pennsylvania.

Ari guessed they were in Beverly Hills when the scenery transformed from concrete sidewalks to lush, green lawns and from high-rises to mansions.

Malcolm checked his watch. "It didn't

take long to get here from the airport. Just about thirty minutes."

They were in the heart of Beverly Hills, only steps from renowned Rodeo Drive. Ari drank in the beauty of the DePaul Hotel. "Wow," he murmured. "Dad, this now belongs to you."

Malcolm's faint smile held a touch of sadness. "Welcome to the DePaul Beverly Hills Hotel," a young man said as they exited the limo. "Miss Rivera will escort you to your meeting."

A young woman with blond hair and wearing a trendy-looking business suit greeted them within minutes of stepping inside the swanky hotel. "Mr. Goodman is waiting for you in the penthouse," she told them.

Ari took note that the outside of the hotel had been inspired by the Spanish Revival architecture and Mediterranean styling that was so prevalent in Beverly Hills. The interior evoked timeless elegance in sun-drenched colors of gold, salmon, coral and cream.

"Absolutely beautiful," he whispered.

His father agreed. "Looks much better in person than in the magazines."

Ari agreed.

They were taken up to the DePaul residence via private elevator and greeted by a stoic-faced man introduced to them as Franklin.

"He was Mr. DePaul's butler," the young woman explained. She led them into a conference room.

The attorney rose to greet them, but it was the woman behind him who caught Ari's attention immediately. His gaze focused on her face and then moved over her body slowly. Her skin reminded him of a smooth café au lait. There was just a hint of makeup on her face, dark brown eyeliner that enhanced her almond-shaped eyes.

Ira Goodman shook hands with both of them. "I asked Natasha LeBlanc to join us. She is a business consultant who has worked with Robert since she was in college. I think you will find her expertise in this industry invaluable."

Natasha smiled and then extended her hand. "It's very nice to meet you both."

Ari was rendered speechless for a moment by her beauty. He swallowed hard, struggling to recover his voice. "It's a pleasure to meet you, as well," he said finally. Something intense flared through his entrancement.

Their eyes met and held.

Ari cleared his throat softly and then

stepped out of the way. He needed to put some distance between them; he was looking for an escape from the seductive scent of her perfume.

They sat around a large custom-designed conference table. Ari made sure to sit two seats away from Natasha.

"I thought you might be hungry, so I ordered lunch," Ira announced. "It should be here shortly."

Ari glanced over at his father, who kept his face void of emotion.

Ira cleared his throat nervously.

Malcolm took a long sip of water before saying, "Mr. Goodman, I have to admit that I'm surprised by all that's happened. I had no idea that Robert DePaul was my father."

Ira nodded. "I can certainly understand how overwhelming this must be."

"Why didn't he leave his estate to his family?"

Ari could feel Natasha's eyes studying him. He met her gaze, forcing her to look away.

"Robert had a private meeting with his family a few days before he died. He gave them a memorandum outlining his final wishes. I have been Robert's attorney for almost thirty years," Ira stated. "I knew him well enough to know that he had made up

16

his mind, and this was the purpose for the meeting. He wanted his relatives to respect his decision in appointing you to replace him at the empire's helm. Robert didn't want knives drawn for his ten-billion-dollar empire."

"Surely he left something for his family," Malcolm said.

Ira nodded. "He did. He handed each of his nephews a two-million-dollar purse, and he set aside trusts for their children. All of the distributions are outlined in a copy of the memorandum before you. In addition to the rest of his estate, he also left a letter for you, which I believe will give you the answers you're seeking. Robert was a very thorough man when it came to matters like these. He never left anything to chance."

Malcolm took the letter but didn't open it.

Ari knew that his father would wait until he was alone to read the note.

"Mr. Alexander, I can only imagine how overwhelmed you must feel right now," Natasha said. "Since Robert's death, the hospitality industry is wondering what's going to happen with the hotels. The employees are concerned, as well. There are a lot of unanswered questions."

Malcolm nodded in understanding.

She took a deep breath and released it. "I'm sure you'd like to take some time to adjust to all of your newfound wealth, however . . ."

"Do you have someone interested in the hotels?" Ari interjected, having a sense of where Natasha was taking the conversation.

She boldly met his gaze. "Although Mr. Alexander hasn't asked my opinion, I do feel that it would be in his best interest to sell the hotels."

"Why?" Ari asked. "Is it because you don't think he can manage the chain? You may not know this, but my family has worked in the hospitality industry for over forty years."

"I am well aware of the *two* hotels owned by your father. The DePaul Hotel & Spa Resorts are a chain of luxury resorts, and it takes —"

"Miss LeBlanc," Ari said, cutting her off, "we are quite capable of taking over the properties. Like you, I'm sure Robert DePaul did his research before deciding to leave his estate to my father. I'm sure we all can agree that he was a very smart businessman." Natasha LeBlanc was extremely beautiful, but he couldn't excuse the condescending tone in her voice.

They were interrupted by a knock.

Franklin stood in the doorway with a cart

laden with food. He carried plates to the table, two at a time. Moving about the room in a nonintrusive manner, he placed a plate in front of each of them. The stuffed chicken breasts smelled delicious. Ari prayed that his stomach wouldn't protest too loudly.

Franklin left the room without making a sound.

"Mr. Alexander, it was not my intention to offend you," Natasha said.

"Your suggestion that my father sell the properties left to him by his father wasn't meant to be offensive?" Ari asked, leaning forward in his seat. *"Are you kidding me?"*

"Son, let it go," Malcolm said quietly.

Ari shook his head. "Dad, I'm sorry, but I can't. Miss LeBlanc took one look at us and decided that we weren't good enough for the DePaul image." He gave her a hard stare. "Admit it. You think we're just a bunch of country bumpkins who don't have a clue when it comes to running a chain of luxury hotels."

Natasha's lips parted in surprise. "I know all about your family business, Mr. Alexander."

"Mr. Alexander is my father. Just call me Ari."

"All right," she responded calmly. "Ari, I know that you have *some* experience in the hospitality industry, but managing a chain of luxury spa resorts isn't the same as what you're used to doing." Nervously, she moistened her dry lips. "It's a bit more involved."

"Yes, there are some notable differences," Ari said. "But I assure you, I have worked with a hotel chain since I was sixteen, and I was very good at my job. Hotel chains ensure a level of consistency — the hotel operates on a larger scale, but if not managed properly, can feel a bit sterile and corporate. Our experience with a smaller hotel allows for a more personal touch. Robert DePaul successfully merged the two, by catering to each guest as if they were the only guest in the hotel."

Natasha nodded in agreement. "I see that you've done your homework."

Ari met her gaze straight on. "I studied Robert DePaul's business model in college. I am well acquainted with the organizational structure of the DePaul Group."

He studied her face for a moment to see if her expression would change, but it remained the same.

Ira gestured toward the woman who had escorted them to the suite. "My assistant will get you a full accounting of Robert's assets."

"Thank you," Malcolm responded.

Ari stole a peek at Natasha.

She was dressed to perfection in a cream-colored, sleeveless silk shirt and a teal-colored pencil skirt. The matching jacket hung on the back of her chair. Natasha was slender, but with an athletic build. She wore her shoulder-length hair in soft curls around her heart-shaped face.

Ari couldn't deny that Natasha was very beautiful, but he didn't like what she was trying to do to his father. Unconsciously, he played with the gold wedding band on his finger.

Ari Alexander resembled his father. They had the same muscular build, and both stood about five or six inches taller than Natasha's five-foot-six-inch frame; Ari's skin was the color of pure honey, while his father was more of a tawny color. They had both inherited those deep, penetrating gray eyes from Robert DePaul. Natasha's gaze halted at the gleaming gold band on his left ring finger.

He's married, Natasha thought with disappointment. She found herself wondering what type of woman he had married. Was she a stay-at-home wife, or did she work in some sort of professional capacity?

Why do I care?

Natasha shook all thoughts of Ari out of her mind and focused on her purpose. She was here to consult on the hotel properties, but also to help Harold DePaul keep what should rightfully belong to him. She just never expected to see such a handsome and virile man standing before her.

Her thoughts centered on Malcolm Alexander. He was not at all as she'd imagined. He didn't seem impressed by all of the luxury surrounding him, and it didn't seem to matter that he was the heir to billions. In fact, Malcolm didn't appear to be thrilled at all about the fact that he was now a very wealthy man.

I'd be the happiest woman alive if I were in his shoes, Natasha thought to herself. She wasn't all about money, but there were times when one desperately needed it for survival.

Her eyes traveled to Ari. Unlike his father, Natasha could tell he really wanted what would one day be his inheritance. He was champing at the bit to get his hands on the hotel properties.

Ari looked at her, his jaw clenched and his eyes slightly narrowed.

Natasha gave him a tiny smile and then quickly looked away, embarrassed that he'd caught her watching him.

She clamped her jaw tight and stared straight ahead. *Why did he have to be so good-looking?*

Natasha could feel him watching her, and she wondered what he was thinking. She heard Ira mention her name and turned her attention to him. "I'm sorry, could you repeat your question?"

The assistant quickly strolled across the carpet and stepped into the hallway. She returned a few minutes later to say, "Ira, you have an urgent call . . ."

"Why don't we take a five-minute break?" the attorney suggested as he made his way to the door.

Ari stood up and walked out of the room. He took a seat in the living room and turned on the television.

Natasha was relieved. She needed some time to get herself together before she looked like a bumbling idiot.

When she returned, Ira walked over to her. "What's going on with you? You okay?"

She stole a peek at Ari, who was walking into the conference room behind his father. "Nothing's going on. Just didn't think this meeting would turn so contentious."

"Natasha, I have a tremendous amount of respect for you, so I'm going to offer a word of advice," Ira said. "Make sure that you are choosing the right side in this battle. Robert knew exactly what he was doing when he left most of his estate to Malcolm Alexander. I'm surprised you would believe otherwise."

Before she could respond, Ira walked over to where Malcolm was standing.

She took a deep breath and then released it slowly. Convincing Malcolm Alexander to sell wasn't going to be an easy feat.

Ari sat with his jaw clenched. When he met her gaze, the line of his mouth tightened a fraction more. He rose to his feet and walked over to the counter to grab an apple.

He picked up a newspaper from the stack lying atop a cabinet. "Secret Son Inherits Robert DePaul's Dynasty," he read aloud. "I guess news travels fast in this town."

"Put that down," Malcolm said. "No matter how big or how small a city, people love to talk."

"It says here that the outraged members of DePaul's family demand a DNA test be performed to prove that you somehow defrauded Robert. Dad, this is crazy," Ari uttered, shaking his head in disgust. "You've never met the man."

A muscle flicked angrily in Malcolm's jaw. "Son, they don't care about that. When

24

people think they have been mistreated, they jump to all sorts of wild conclusions. They are looking to blame someone — anyone. They can say whatever they feel, but it doesn't make it true. This applies to Robert DePaul, as well. For all we know, he could've done all this to upset his family. I have no problem with taking a DNA test. I think we all want to know the truth."

"Robert was very clear," the attorney said as he entered the room. "He wanted to acknowledge you as his only ch—"

Malcolm cut him off by saying, "My mother never once mentioned this man. Frankly, I don't know how or when she could've met him. This could be a case of mistaken identity."

Ira pointed to the letter Malcolm was holding. "I believe the letter you have in your hand will give you the answers you need."

"I want to have the DNA test," Malcolm blurted. His tone brooked no argument.

"I think you're making a wise decision, Mr. Alexander," Natasha interjected.

"Dad, you don't have to do this," Ari argued. He gazed at Natasha as he said, "You don't have to prove anything to these people."

Malcolm nodded. "I know, but I want it,

all the same, son. I'm not doing this for them as much as for me."

Ari waited to see if his father would say more, but nothing came. The matter was settled.

CHAPTER 2

After spending over an hour going over an inventory of Robert's real estate holdings, Ira called for another five-minute break. He excused himself to take a phone call. Natasha did the same, leaving Malcolm and Ari alone in the conference room.

Ari stood up to stretch. He had no idea their meeting would take so long. He was tired and his father looked exhausted. They were both still on East Coast time.

Malcolm picked up the unopened letter and said, "I was about eight or nine years old when I asked my mama why I didn't look like any of them."

"What did she tell you?" Ari asked.

"She sat me down and explained that I had a different father. Mama did tell me that he was a white man, and that they had loved each other very much. That's all she told me, and at the time, I guess it was enough for me."

27

"How do you feel about all of this now?" Ari inquired.

Malcolm shrugged. "Son, I'm not sure. First, I want to have that DNA test done, and then we'll just go from there."

Ari pointed to the letter. "Aren't you going to read it?"

"Eventually, but not just yet," his father responded.

"You plan on waiting until after the DNA test results come back?" Ari walked around the room, looking at the artwork. He stopped at a window and peered outside.

Malcolm shook his head. "No, it's addressed to me specifically, so I intend to read it, but I'm just not ready right now." He rose to his feet and joined Ari at the window. "This is a beautiful city."

"It sure is," Ari agreed.

"Dad, Robert DePaul was a brilliant man," he said after a moment. "He wouldn't have left you his estate if he didn't know for sure that you are his son. Take another look at that portrait on the wall behind you. You are the spitting image of him — you just have more coloring. That's why I can't believe a DNA test is needed."

"Ari, there's no shame in taking that test. It will alleviate any issues later."

"Ira told us that the will is ironclad."

28

"To be honest, I'm not worried about it, son. I'm not sure I *want* to be saddled with Robert DePaul's estate. Look at all that stuff on the table. Our lives are not complicated, and to tell you the truth, I prefer to keep it that way."

A muscle quivered in his jaw. Ari couldn't believe what he was hearing. "You are actually considering not accepting the inheritance? Dad, you can't be serious."

"I have always worked for everything I ever had, Ari. I am not going to feud with the DePaul family over this man's money. I never knew Robert DePaul personally, and I don't need his money."

Ari didn't argue, but he didn't believe that his father should refuse the inheritance. He was Robert DePaul's son and legally entitled to his estate.

His parents believed in helping others less fortunate — with that much money, they could really make an impact in their small town. The schools needed books for students. His family had been hosting fundraisers to get the money. Well, the inheritance would enable them to buy textbooks for all of the students. Then, there was Habitat for Humanity. His father wasn't thinking clearly.

"Son, what are you thinking about?"

29

Ari turned his attention to his father. "I was thinking about all the good that could come from you accepting this inheritance. The schools back in Aspen could have textbooks for every student."

Malcolm nodded. "We could build several houses . . . I've considered all of this. Despite it all, I have to consult the good Lord, Ari. Everything we do must be done in order. God is the ultimate counselor, and it's his advice I will seek."

Ari couldn't argue with that, so he remained quiet.

Natasha paused a moment outside the door of the residence to straighten her jacket. She ran her fingers through her dark brown, shoulder-length hair.

"This is definitely not going to be as easy as I thought," she whispered. Ari Alexander had taken an instant dislike to her the moment she opened her mouth. Now she had to find a way to do damage control.

I can't come on too strong, she thought. *It will only make them suspicious.*

Natasha took a deep breath and released it slowly. She allowed the tension to leave her body before she entered the residence. She was never this nervous around clients.

Ari was in the living room when she

strolled into the foyer. He eyed her a moment before saying, "I see you're back, Miss LeBlanc."

Her back stiffened at the coolness of his words. "Did you assume I wouldn't return?" she asked, noting that his gray eyes were like silver lightning.

"I am smart enough to never *assume* anything where you're concerned," Ari replied. He checked his watch and then said, "We should join the others."

Irritated, Natasha glared at his back as she followed him into the conference room. When they were all seated, she pulled out a proposal. "Mr. Alexander, this is a copy of an offer from another corporation interested in acquiring the five-star properties."

Malcolm picked up the proposal but didn't open it. "I will review the offer and then get back to you with my answer," he told her.

Natasha had expected this response from Malcolm. She also expected the stern expression that graced Ari's face.

"May I have a word with you, Miss LeBlanc?" Ari inquired.

"Sure," she responded with a tiny smile. Natasha struggled to appear calm, but deep inside her stomach was filled with nervous energy. She half expected Malcolm to intervene, but he remained silent.

Ari led her into another room.

"Tell me something. What's in this for you?" he asked, openly studying her face, as if trying to read her thoughts.

Her eyebrows rose in surprise. "Excuse me?"

"Let's not play games," Ari snapped in frustration. "What will you get if you are able to convince my father to sell? What's in it for you?"

Natasha struggled to keep her voice low. "I'm afraid I don't know what you're talking about."

"C'mon, I wasn't born yesterday," Ari uttered. "You definitely have something to gain, or you wouldn't be working so hard otherwise. Who wants to buy hotels from my father?"

"It's a conglomerate out of Nevada. They are looking to get into the hospitality industry. Purchasing the DePaul Hotel & Spa Resorts would provide them the opportunity with minimum risk." Natasha settled back in her seat, saying, "I am merely here to look out for your father's best interest. I think their proposal is a sound one. Mr. Alexander stands to make millions off this deal."

Ari folded his arms across his chest. "Miss

LeBlanc, my father doesn't need you to look after him. He has a wife and six children who definitely have his back one hundred percent."

Frustrated, Natasha shook her head. *How could a man look so sexy and be so irritating at the same time?* She carefully considered her words. "Ari, I'd really like for us to be on the same side. This is why Ira asked me to meet with you and Mr. Alexander. I am merely suggesting that your father consider all options."

"No, you're not," Ari argued. "You are pushing for him to sell the properties. As long as you're trying to force my father to sell what is rightfully his, we will never be on the same side."

She folded her arms across her chest. "I haven't known your father for very long, but from what I've seen, I can't force him to do anything." Natasha paused a moment before adding, "And neither can you. Now, if you're done, I'd like to rejoin our meeting."

Her cell phone rang.

She answered and said, "I need to call you back. Give me ten minutes."

"Why don't you take your call now?" Ari suggested. "There are some questions I have for Ira. I can discuss them while you're

33

returning your phone call."

Natasha glared at him before heading to the door. She could feel the heat of his gaze on her body.

In the hallway, she slowed down her breathing as she stepped into the elevator, forcing her body to relax. Natasha went down to the lobby.

She waited until she was out of the building before pulling out her phone.

"I didn't mean to be so abrupt, but I was having a conversation with Malcolm's son," she said when Harold DePaul answered his phone.

"How is it going?" he asked.

"I did as you instructed, but I think you might have a problem."

"I'm listening."

"Malcolm Alexander is willing to take a DNA test. Harold, he is the spitting image of your uncle," Natasha stated. "He *is* Robert's son."

Harold muttered something unintelligible.

"As much as the thought may detest you, Malcolm *is* a part of your family. It may be better to embrace him rather than become his enemy."

"I just want what should rightfully and lawfully be mine — Uncle Robert's estate," Harold blurted. "I gave that man nothing but years of loyalty and dedication. He owes Malcolm Alexander nothing."

Natasha didn't agree but decided to keep her mouth shut. Harold DePaul had always been temperamental, a man who wanted to have everything his way. Although he and Robert often butted heads, they respected one another.

"I did what you asked me to do and left the proposal with Malcolm," Natasha responded. "Just so you know, his son doesn't want the properties sold. I'm not sure how much influence Ari has on his father, but he could be a problem."

"Use your charm," Harold suggested. "I'm sure a beautiful woman such as yourself can convince the man to do what is right."

Natasha struggled to keep her temper in check. "I don't work this way, and *you know it.*"

Harold was silent for a moment then responded, "I'm sorry, Natasha. I shouldn't have said that."

"No, you shouldn't have," she said tersely. "I told you from the very beginning that I would help you, but only if everything was aboveboard. I haven't changed my mind about that. I am not going to do anything illegal."

"The initial payment has been made," Harold blurted. "This should put a smile on your pretty little face."

"It doesn't matter if you're planning to play dirty," Natasha replied, standing her ground. "You can have all of the money back if you try to change the terms of our agreement."

"Natasha, I know that you need me as much as I need you right now, so let's just try to get along," Harold suggested. "We used to be good friends, you and me."

"Until you showed your true colors," she responded.

"I never meant to hurt you."

"I don't want to talk about it, Harold. Leave the past in the past."

"I have faith in you, Natasha. You can convince Malcolm Alexander to do the right thing. We can't let that hillbilly family mess up everything my uncle and I worked for. Those people have no clue how to run a multimillion-dollar-a-year luxury resort, much less a chain of them. Two insignificant hotels does not make a chain."

"I will do what I can to help you, Harold."

"That's all I ask of you, Natasha."

She ended the call and put away her cell phone. "I hope I'm doing the right thing," Natasha whispered. She had no idea why

Robert DePaul gave everything to a son he had never met, but she assumed it was mostly out of guilt.

He had spoken of his love for Malcolm's mother, and his regret of not having a relationship with his son. Robert had confessed that he had loved Pearle Alexander more than he had ever loved another woman, including his late wife.

Still, Natasha was shocked over the news that the majority of the estate would go to Malcolm and not Harold.

Malcolm Alexander was not a man moved by money. Harold, on the other hand, enjoyed living a lavish lifestyle. He frequented star-studded galas, movie premieres, award shows and parties — he wanted to be on the Hollywood A-list. Robert DePaul loved the finer things in life, as well, but he was a very generous man who preferred to stay out of the limelight.

Ari watched as the lab tech swabbed the inside of Malcolm's cheek. Ira had arranged for the DNA test to be done immediately, per his father's request.

"You didn't have to do this," he told his father after the tech left the room. "Robert DePaul's instructions were clear. If anyone in his family challenged his will, they would forfeit their share in his inheritance," Ari stated. "Their portion would automatically revert to you. The man made sure his will was ironclad."

"This is not about them," Malcolm stated. "They have every right to be concerned, but I'm doing this for me. I thought you understood, son."

"I hear what you're saying, Dad," Ari responded. "I just don't get it. Do you really think Robert DePaul would've left you anything if he were not sure that you are his son?"

"We see the similarity now, but only because we're looking for it," Malcolm responded. "How many times have we looked at DePaul's picture and never noticed that we have his eyes?"

"You're right," Ari muttered while staring at the huge portrait of his newly discovered grandfather. His dad was right. He had never seen the resemblance before news of the inheritance surfaced.

Ira and his assistant stepped outside the room.

"Dad, what are you afraid of?" Ari inquired when it was just the two of them.

Malcolm frowned. "What are you talking about?"

"You haven't opened the letter yet. Why?"

"Because I know that everything I've ever believed is going to change. I'm not so sure that I'm ready for that."

Ari broke into a grin. "Grandma adored you. That will never change. You and Grandpa — the relationship you had with him will never change."

"Son, why is keeping this inheritance so important to you?"

"Because this is a chance to help our Aspen community in a way that we've always talked about. We talked about owning a chain of hotels . . . this just feels right to me, Dad. I will respect your decision, whatever choice you make."

"We will hear what the rest of the family has to say," Malcolm said.

Ari's eyes traveled around the room. "Robert DePaul certainly had good taste. This is probably the best-looking conference room I've ever been in."

Malcolm agreed.

"Is Natasha still on that call?" Ari asked. He wondered briefly if she were talking with the people wanting to purchase the hotel properties. Probably giving them an update, he decided. His father was a very intelligent man and had a head for business. He would not be easily swayed one way or the other.

"Must be." His father pushed away from

the table and stood up.

Franklin appeared with a tray of bottles decorated with Swarovski crystals.

Malcolm glanced over at Ari, who asked, "What are those?"

"Bottled water, sir," Franklin replied.

"That's some fancy bottle," Malcolm commented as he took one. "Bling H_2O. I never heard of this. Have you, son?"

"No, I haven't." Ari picked up his cell phone and began typing. "Franklin, would you happen to know how much one of these would cost? I'm just curious."

"They run anywhere from thirty-eight a bottle to thousands of dollars. It really depends on the type of bottle, sir."

Malcolm shook his head in disbelief. "Designer water . . ."

"It's the Cristal of bottled water," Ari interjected, reading from the web browser on his iPhone. "It was created by a Hollywood producer. The water contained in the bottle comes from a Tennessee spring."

"Mister Robert only allowed Bling H_2O to be served at his hotels," the butler contributed. "However, he kept King Island Cloud Juice stocked for select VIP guests." He paused a moment before adding, "Will this be all, sir?"

"Yes. Thank you, Franklin." Malcolm

examined the bottle of water. "This is too pretty to drink. I'm going to have to take a bottle home to your mama. I can't wait to see the expression on her face."

Ari chuckled. His mother would never believe it without seeing the bottle of luxury water for herself.

Malcolm poured the chilled liquid into a glass and took a sip. "It tastes good," he said. "Almost too good to be true."

Ari followed suit. "I have to say that this is the best water I've ever tasted. I thought Le Bleu was expensive at twelve dollars a bottle."

His father nodded in agreement. "We only carry Le Bleu Premium when a customer requests it, and even then, they pay for it. This is certainly a different lifestyle."

"It would take some getting used to," Ari said. "Don't know about you, but I'm up to the challenge."

Natasha strolled into the room. "I apologize for having to interrupt our meeting, but that call had been scheduled for months."

"It's quite all right," Malcolm responded. "You haven't missed much."

Ari leaned forward in his chair. "So you and Robert were *close*."

"Not in the way that you are implying,"

she responded coldly. "Robert was my mentor when I was in college, and I worked for him before starting my own consulting company. I was just as close to his wife before she passed away."

"Son, stop giving this little lady a hard time."

Natasha smiled smoothly, betraying nothing of her annoyance.

Ari looked at his father. "Miss LeBlanc looks like she can take care of herself, Dad. She doesn't need your protection."

Ira strode back into the conference room with purpose. "I need to get back to my office for a meeting," he announced. "Let's table the rest for tomorrow."

Malcolm gave a slight nod. "That's fine."

Natasha rose to her feet. "It has truly been a pleasure to meet you, Mr. Alexander."

"What about me?" Ari asked.

"It was nice to meet you, too," she responded. "I'll see you both in the morning."

"We're not going anywhere." Ari smiled when he caught the expression on Natasha's face. The meaning behind his words hadn't escaped her.

CHAPTER 3

Ari Alexander was infuriating, to say the least. What had she done to make him so distrustful of her? Natasha drove along the 405 freeway, trying to figure out the answer to that question.

"I'm doing the right thing," she kept telling herself over and over again. Natasha thought about her last conversation with Robert. He had been clear about his final instructions — this much she knew. Robert DePaul died the very next day.

The last thing she wanted to do was betray the man who had been a mentor to her, but in some ways she could understand why Harold felt so slighted. He had worked alongside his uncle and been extremely loyal to Robert. Malcolm appeared to be a good man, but he had never had any type of relationship with his biological father.

Natasha didn't want to insult Malcolm Alexander or his infuriating son, but she hoped that they would seriously consider her advice to sell, although she didn't mention that the investment group interested consisted of members of Robert DePaul's family.

Shortly after the will was read, Harold approached her with a way for his family to retain the hotel group. She didn't see any reason not to help him — Harold and his relatives only wanted to protect what should have been theirs in the first place.

Despite Malcolm's business acumen, Natasha still believed that he lacked the experience for running a hotel chain of this size. Once Malcolm decided to sell, Harold promised to pay her the balance of the money they offered. Medical bills would eat up the ten thousand Robert left her. He had also given her complete ownership of the building that housed her company. If Harold hadn't approached her with his offer, she had planned to sell the building.

She put on her right signal as she switched lanes. Natasha was taking the next off-ramp. She was looking forward to slipping off her heels and relaxing. It had been a trying day, to say the least.

Ari and his father escorted Ira and his assistant to the door.

"I'm only a phone call away," Ira told them. "Call if you have any questions."

"There won't be anything pressing that can't wait until morning," Malcolm responded.

Ari settled down in the living room and turned on the television. Malcolm was about to join him when Franklin appeared from another room.

"The master bedroom has been prepared for you, Mr. Alexander." He turned to Ari and said, "You will be in the guest room across the hall."

"Thank you," they said in unison.

"Mr. Alexander, is there anything I can get for you before dinner?" Franklin inquired.

"We're fine," Malcolm said.

"Chef Ricardo will have dinner prepared promptly at 6:00 p.m."

There was a thin smile on his lips as Malcolm gave a slight nod. "Thank you."

Franklin disappeared as quietly as he had arrived.

"That dude bothers me," Ari whispered. "I wonder if he even knows how to smile. Maybe it's in the Butlers of America handbook or something that smiling is strictly forbidden."

Laughing, Malcolm nodded in agreement.

"I don't know how Robert could have him lurking around all of the time. Ira told me that Franklin and Chef Ricardo actually live across the hall in accommodations for personal staff. However, he moved into the room near the kitchen when Robert got sick. He was very loyal to Robert."

Ari gave his father a sidelong glance and said in a loud whisper, "Well, now he's yours."

Malcolm sighed softly. He got up and walked into the conference room. He returned a few minutes later carrying the letter from Robert. "I guess I should read this now."

"You don't have to do it until you're ready," Ari told him. "Maybe you should wait until you're with Mom."

"I thought about that, but I changed my mind," Malcolm said. "I guess my curiosity is getting the better of me."

They sat down at the table, side by side.

Malcolm opened the letter. He read the words aloud.

Malcolm,
I'm sure the news that you are my son has blindsided you and for that, I apologize. I have long wanted to come to you, but your mother made me promise never to disrupt

your life.

I met Pearle Strickland in Wilmington, North Carolina, when she worked as a housekeeper for the DePaul DeSoto Hotel owned by my family. I want you to know that Pearle and I were very much in love, but we were both concerned with how our relationship would be viewed by the world and our families.

When Pearle found out that she was pregnant, she decided it was best to spare my family the scandal by leaving town. This was not what I wanted, but I'm sure you are aware of your mother's stubborn streak — she would have it no other way.

Soon after, I received word that she was getting married and she urged me to forget about her. She told me that Theodore Alexander was a good man and would be a good father to you. She insisted that this was the way it had to be. I was to never have any contact with you.

Although this was what your mother wanted, I found it hard not to keep track of how you were progressing. My wife and I were never fortunate to have children. I have always believed God would not allow me another child because I had not honored the one he blessed me with. Malcolm, I want you to understand that this is not about my guilt in not publicly recognizing you as my son.

It is no accident that you are in the hospitality business. Your mother had always shown an interest in her own hotel, and I was happy to teach her everything I knew at the time. I believe she used the money I had given her when she left to purchase the small inn she owned. She and her husband transformed what was virtually nothing into a very successful bed-and-breakfast.

Then you returned home from the military and opened the first Alexander Hotel. Five years later, the second one opened, and that's when I knew that you were the one who would carry the DePaul Hotel Group into the future. You have the vision and the business acumen I desire in a successor. Vision is the most powerful thing owned by any human being, even stronger than financial power. With you at the helm, I expect our modus operandi will continue harmoniously as we have done in the past.

Despite all you will hear about me, the one thing I want you to know for sure — I was just a man who loved a woman, but was foolish enough to allow others to keep me away from her. For that, I am deeply ashamed.

I hope one day you will find it in your heart to forgive me. Although we never had as much as a conversation, I have always loved you as a son. If only God had granted me a few more years. I did not want to come to you as an ill man.

I will leave this earth in peace, knowing that I have finally corrected a grievous wrong. You are the future of the DePaul Hotel Group.

Your father,
Robert DePaul

"So, what do you think?" Ari questioned half in anticipation, half in dread as he silently observed a range of emotions that had settled on his father's face.

Malcolm shrugged. "If Robert DePaul wanted a relationship with me, he could have had one, regardless of how my mother felt. All he had to do was acknowledge me as his son. What could she have done?" He folded the letter carefully and stuck it back into the envelope.

"I get the feeling he didn't want to embarrass Grandma." Ari met his father's gaze. "I do believe that he wanted to have a relationship with you, though."

Malcolm didn't seem convinced. "His wife never gave him children. If she had, do you

49

really think he would have left his estate to me?"

Ari didn't know the answer to that, but he replied, "He didn't have to leave it to you, Dad. He could've left it to his DePaul relatives."

"Maybe he should have," Malcolm uttered.

"Dad, don't say that."

"I don't need his money."

"But he wanted you to have it," Ari countered. "Dad, you are his son and he made sure that you were taken care of — I think it's admirable."

"Or misplaced guilt," Malcolm contributed. "He made a choice a long time ago, and he should have left it at that."

"You're angry," Ari told his father.

The tense lines on Malcolm's face relaxed. "My life was fine, and I'm not so sure I'm willing to give it up for a three-ring circus."

Ari nodded in understanding. His father was a private man, and his inheritance had thrust him into the limelight.

"Dad, legally you are entitled to everything Robert DePaul left you, and I think it's an incredible blessing. You and Mom have always talked about owning a chain of hotels — you can do that now. Dad, this is in our blood."

"Your mother and I will pray over this situation. The good Lord above will guide us in making the right decision."

Ari agreed.

The butler arrived to announce that dinner was being served, and he led them to the dining room.

"Is someone joining us?" Malcolm asked, looking at the beautiful display of food on the table.

"It will just be the two of you," the butler replied.

"This is a lot of food," Ari interjected. The delectable spread included roast chicken, baked tilapia, steamed vegetables, rice pilaf and assorted rolls.

Malcolm agreed. "Tell Chef Ricardo to come on out here. You two will eat with us. The best way to get to know a person is over a meal, I always say."

Franklin looked shocked but managed to recover. "Sir . . ."

"Call me Malcolm. The first thing I want you to know about me is that I'm a simple man. Now, there's no way that my son and I can eat up all of this food, so y'all come join us. We don't believe in wasting food."

Franklin swallowed hard and then gave a slight nod. "We'd be honored, sir."

He left the room, walking quickly.

51

Ari looked at his father and grinned. "I thought the man was about to pass out when you asked him to eat with us."

Malcolm chuckled as he sat down at the table.

Franklin returned with Chef Ricardo. Both men wore expressions of disbelief and waited for Ari to sit down before seating themselves.

Malcolm said the blessing.

Franklin didn't pick up his fork until Malcolm and Ari sampled the food on their plates.

"Everything is delicious," Malcolm said. He wiped his mouth on the end of his napkin.

Ari agreed.

Chef Ricardo smiled. "It was very nice of you to allow us to join you." He glanced down at his plate. "Franklin and I usually take our meals in the kitchen."

"You went through a lot of effort to cook this fancy meal," Malcolm acknowledged, "so I figure you might as well enjoy some of it with us."

"Forgive me for staring," Franklin murmured. "You look so much like Mr. Robert. He was a very kind man, although sad at times. He spoke of your mother often."

Malcolm gave a polite smile. "I regret that

I will never have the chance to meet or get to know Robert DePaul. I have always admired his business acumen."

"Franklin, how did you come to work for Robert?" Ari asked while cutting into the tender fish.

"I was living on the streets," Franklin said. "One day when I was looking for food, I saw these thugs trying to rob Mr. Robert. I went to help him." He stuck a forkful of vegetables into his mouth.

"Franklin is a black belt in karate," Chef Ricardo interjected.

"I made sure Mr. Robert made it safely to his car. When he was inside, I was about to walk off, and he called me back. I thought he was going to offer me some money, but he offered me a job instead," Franklin said. "That was almost eight years ago."

Ari glanced over at Ricardo, who said, "I met Mr. Robert at the World Culinary Showcase in Dallas, Texas. He came up to me after my presentation and invited me to lunch. A faculty member from the school I attended told him about me. He flew me out here to cook a meal for him and his wife. They loved it and offered me a permanent position as their personal chef. I have been with them for five years now."

"Mr. Robert was a good man," Franklin

said. "I am sorry you didn't get the chance to meet him personally."

"Me, too," Malcolm responded.

For dessert, there was lemon pound cake with strawberries and whipped cream and a chocolate drizzle.

Later, Ari settled down to watch some television while his father was in the master bedroom on the telephone.

He's talking to Mom, Ari thought silently. He hoped that his mother could convince his father to keep the inheritance. This was a once-in-a-lifetime chance for his parents to live out their dreams.

Ari's thoughts centered on Natasha; he couldn't understand how she evoked feelings he thought long dead. The way she looked at him, even when he felt the heat of her frustration . . . she affected him deeply, and it bothered him.

I don't trust her.

She was loyal to Robert. Did that mean she was just as loyal to the rest of his family?

Natasha was glad to be home. She kicked off her shoes as soon as she entered the trendy three-bedroom condo. Natasha removed her jacket next.

A full-figured woman wearing a T-shirt and jeans came down the stairs carrying an empty glass.

Natasha smiled. "How did today go, Monica?"

"It was a good day," she responded with a smile.

They talked for a few minutes before Natasha headed upstairs to a bedroom. She entered the room. "Hey, you," she greeted.

A little boy sitting at a desk in front of a computer looked up and grinned. "Mommy, you're home."

"I sure am. Nurse Monica told me that you had a good day." Joshua was her pride and joy. Natasha tickled his ears.

He giggled. "I did."

"How was class today?" she asked. Her six-year-old son had leukemia, and for the moment he was in remission. He wasn't able to go to school because his blood counts were low, putting him at risk for infection. Joshua was able to keep up with his friends and class work via satellite.

"Kinda boring," Joshua responded. "I have homework to do."

"Is that what you're working on?"

Joshua nodded. "I have to write a story about a fish."

She gave him a sidelong glance. "You love fish, don't you?"

"But I don't want to write about a fish,"

Joshua stated. "I want to write a story about football."

"Well, why don't you email Mrs. Terry and ask if you can do that?" Natasha suggested.

He smiled. "Okay, I will."

He had been looking forward to playing football this summer with a Pop Warner league. He was finally old enough for the flag football team that practiced at the park a block away from their building. But in a cruel twist of fate, Joshua was diagnosed with leukemia.

She hugged him. "I love you, Joshua."

"I love you more."

"You work on that email to your teacher while I change into something comfortable."

"Can we have spaghetti for dinner?" Joshua asked.

"We sure can," she responded with a grin. Joshua loved spaghetti and would eat it every night if she let him.

Natasha stood in the doorway of his room, gazing at him. When Joshua was diagnosed a few months ago, his doctor had informed her that he needed to be out of school for one to three years because the chemotherapy treatments would compromise his immune system. It didn't take much for Joshua to get sick. Just last week, they had to run back and forth to the hospital because Joshua kept running a temperature.

She'd exhausted her savings just to hire Monica so that Joshua had a full-time nurse. Her insurance hadn't made a dent in the mountain of medical bills sitting on her desk. Robert fell ill a month before she received Joshua's diagnosis, so she hadn't confided in him. She was grateful for the ten thousand he left for her, but that wouldn't cover future treatments. When Harold approached her with the offer to pay the medical bills in full, she'd jumped at the opportunity. Nothing was more important to her than Joshua.

CHAPTER 4

"So, this is where Robert spent his final days," Ari said when they ventured into the master bedroom. "This place looks fit for a king."

Malcolm glanced around the large bedroom. "I guess to some, Robert DePaul was a king."

Ari navigated around the bedroom. "Dad, this is spectacular. This closet is big enough to make me dizzy, and there's another room in here with a washer and dryer."

Malcolm frowned. "A washer and dryer in the bedroom? I've never heard of such."

"I guess they make bedrooms more functional out here in California. If I had a bedroom like this, I could get a whole day's work done without ever leaving the room."

Ari strolled into another room. "There is a subzero freezer and fridge in here, too. This definitely works for me."

"And to think, all your mother and I ever

dreamed of having in our bedroom is a fireplace," Malcolm said.

"Well, now you have two fireplaces, a wide-screen television and a waterfall in the shower built for two." Ari walked over to his father and said, "Dad, I hope you and Mom know what to do with all this stuff."

Malcolm grinned. "Don't worry about us, son. I'm sure we could figure it out."

"Dad, you and Mom deserve to live like this. You two have worked so hard for the family. I'm glad Robert left his estate to you. It was the right thing to do, but also he made the right decision. You will bring nothing but honor to his legacy."

The two men embraced.

Malcolm stifled a yawn. "I don't know about you, but I'm still on East Coast time. I'm beat."

"I am, too," Ari said. "I'll see you in the morning."

He left the master suite and walked across the hall where he would be sleeping. His suite was not as opulent as the bedroom his father was in, but it was the largest guest room Ari had ever been in. His master retreat at home was a nice size but definitely not this big.

Ari made his way to the bathroom and turned on the shower. "You can fit two people in this one, too," he whispered. "Man, this is nice."

He showered, slipped into a pair of pajamas and settled down in the sitting room to watch television. A picture of April formed in Ari's mind.

She's smiling. This must mean that she's happy and at peace.

Ari missed her dearly. He touched the wedding band on his finger as his heart grieved the loss of the only woman he had ever loved. He often wondered if he would ever feel such emotion for another person again.

Another image formed.

His breath caught as Natasha's faced loomed in his mind. Ari shook his head as if trying to shake the likeness of her out of his mind. How could she control his thoughts like this? Everything about Natasha disturbed him.

After a dinner of spaghetti and turkey meatballs, Natasha helped Joshua with his homework and then read him a story. Joshua had complained of feeling tired afterward, so he had gone straight to bed.

Natasha settled down in her den and opened a novel. She found it hard to concentrate on reading. Ari Alexander and his father dominated her thoughts. They didn't have the experience needed to manage luxury properties like the DePaul Hotel Group. *Why can't Ari see that?*

Harold had worked under Robert's tutelage since college. He was more qualified, and he was Robert's nephew. *But Malcolm Alexander was Robert's son.*

"This is such a mess," she whispered. It was too bad they couldn't find some way to work together. Harold had been the one balking at the very thought of joining forces with Malcolm. He wanted all of Robert's assets retained in their family.

Natasha wasn't sure how this situation was going to turn out, but she prayed for a positive outcome. She liked and respected Malcolm Alexander. His son Ari was another story, however.

Those deep, penetrating eyes of his seemed to look right through Natasha. His gaze was uncomfortable and kept her on the defensive.

He thinks I'm trying to cheat his father out of his fortune, but I'm protecting him, Natasha kept telling herself. *Besides, this really has nothing to do with Ari. It's Malcolm's decision. Enough about Ari,* she silently chided. *He's a married man and after tomorrow, I probably won't ever see him again.*

61

Natasha stifled a yawn. She was exhausted, but it was much too early for her to go to bed.

She rose to her feet and made her way to her son's room.

Joshua was asleep.

Natasha stood there, watching him. She was so proud of her little angel. Since finding out about the leukemia, Joshua had exhibited nothing but courage, even at his weakest.

Whenever he went in to have chemo, Joshua was always the one trying to cheer up the others who were scared or sobbing. He liked to make cards for the other children in the hospital, or take them candy.

Natasha felt something wet on her cheeks. She hadn't realized she was crying. She wiped her face on the back of her hands and then eased the door shut. She quietly made her way to her bedroom and turned on the monitor. It gave her comfort, knowing that she could hear her son cry out if he needed her.

The telephone rang.

She saw her sister's name on the caller ID and picked up the receiver.

"Natalie," she said into the phone. "It's about time you called me back. Mama's been driving me crazy about your engagement dinner. Remember how she was when Nathan got married? Well, she is even worse now." She glanced over at a photo of the three of them. They were triplets and very close.

Her sister laughed. "I'm sorry. My case-load is really heavy right now. I've been trying to clear my desk before the wedding."

"I understand, but our mother doesn't. You know she wants everything to be perfect."

"It will be," Natalie responded. "She just needs to relax. How's my little sweetie?"

"He had a good day today, sis. He was tired after dinner, so I sent him to bed."

"I know deep down that Joshua is going to be fine," Natalie stated. "Just let me know if I can help you with money, doctors . . . anything."

"We are going to be fine, I think," Natasha said. "I feel so much better having a full-time nurse caring for him when I'm not here."

"That has to be expensive."

"It is," Natasha confirmed. "But I'll do whatever I have to do for Joshua."

"Have you heard from his father?" her sister asked.

"No, and I don't expect to hear from him. Natalie, the man that was supposed to love me forever . . . he left me for a stripper. Calvin never wanted to be a father, so when I got pregnant — that was the last straw for him."

"I never thought he was good enough for you, Natasha. You know I never liked him."

"I know. Back then I couldn't understand why, but I do now." She ran her fingers through her hair, fingering the curls. "Let's talk about you. My sister's getting married."

"I am," she squealed on the other end of the line.

"I'm really happy for you, Natalie, but I have to confess that I'm a tiny bit jealous. I want a happily ever after."

"You're going to get yours," Natalie assured her. "The right man is on his way to you."

An image of Ari formed in her mind, but Natasha shooed it away. *He's a married man,* she silently screamed.

"Natasha, you still here?"

She forced her thoughts back to her conversation with her sister. "Yeah, I'm here."

They talked for almost two hours before Natasha said, "Natalie, I can't wait to see you this weekend." She glanced over at the clock and said, "Sweetie, I have a meeting tomorrow morning, so I need to get ready for bed."

"Give the munchkin a big hug for me."

"I will," she promised.

Natasha hung up the phone and then went to check on Joshua one more time. She sat down in the chair beside his bed, watching him as a smile tugged at her lips.

Malcolm was in the kitchen pouring a cup of coffee when Ari walked out of the guest bedroom. "Want some?" he asked.

"Sure," Ari responded. "Where's Chef Ricardo? I'm sure he'd have a fit to find you helping yourself to coffee. I think it's impolite or something."

Smiling, Malcolm handed him a cup of steaming-hot coffee. "He offered, but I insisted on doing it myself. Ricardo left for a grocery run this morning. Apparently, he takes care of all of the shopping when it comes to the kitchen. He told me that he gets here at 7:00 a.m. and doesn't leave until after seven in the evening. He has weekends off, however."

"How did you sleep?" Ari inquired.

"I slept pretty good. Missed your mother, though."

"I still haven't gotten used to sleeping without April." A wild flash of grief ripped through him. "Dad, I miss her so much."

"She was a wonderful woman." Malcolm took a sip of his coffee. "Oh, the food is already set up in the conference room. We're going to have a working breakfast with Ira and Natasha."

"I don't trust that woman," Ari stated at the mention of Natasha's name.

"Get to know her, son, before you make any assumptions."

Ari eyed his father. "I know you, Dad. You don't trust her any more than I do."

There was a knock on the door.

Ari followed Franklin into the foyer and greeted Ira with a handshake.

Natasha entered the elegantly appointed quarters a few minutes after Ira arrived. Ari felt his pulse involuntarily leap with excitement.

She greeted everyone before saying to Ari, "Good morning. I really hope that we can find some common ground today."

He cleared his throat, pretending not to be affected by her. "My position hasn't changed, Miss LeBlanc."

"I see." She switched her purse from one side to the other. "Well, if you will excuse me, I need to speak to Ira before we get started."

Her perfume attacked his nostrils, casting a spell of seduction. His heartbeat throbbed in his ears. Ari couldn't seem to tear his gaze away as Natasha made confident strides across the marble floor, her hips swaying gently as she walked.

What is wrong with me?

His pulse skittered alarmingly. Ari was knocked off guard by his response to Natasha. Never had he experienced anything so powerful. None of this made much sense to him. He took a few minutes to gather himself before joining the others in the conference room.

Malcolm surveyed his face a moment before asking, "You all right, son?"

Ari ignored the amused look on his father's face and nodded. He sat down beside his father and across from Natasha.

She looked up from the document she had been reading just as he took his seat, but she didn't say a word.

Ira closed the door to the conference room so that they wouldn't be overheard. "I trust you and Ari slept well, Malcolm."

"We did," they responded in unison.

Natasha was the first to speak. "Mr. Alexander, I would like to offer my apologies if I said anything to offend you yesterday. It was not my intent. I had only hoped to offer advice on what should be done in regards to the hotel properties. I never meant to imply that you should rescind your rights to the rest of the estate."

"Miss LeBlanc, you will find that I am not easily offended," Malcolm responded. "My son and I are anxious to return home, so we will make this quick. I am not prepared to make a decision today regarding the estate. When I get home, I intend to discuss it with the rest of my family. As soon as we decide what is best for our family and the DNA results are back, I will meet with you and Ira. You will know what we have decided at that time."

Ari silently noted that Natasha and Ira both looked surprised by his father's response.

After a moment, Natasha said, "I completely understand." She pushed away from the table and said, "I look forward to our next meeting. Safe travels to you, Mr. Alexander, and to you, as well, Ari." She checked her watch. "I have another appointment in an hour, so I really need to get going."

"I'll walk you out," Ari stated as he rose to his feet.

He waited until they were out of the conference room before saying, "It was a pleasure meeting you, Miss LeBlanc." His heartbeat throbbed in his ears.

She looked up at him. *"Really?"*

They halted their steps. "You sound surprised."

"I am, because that's not the impression I got from you."

He was struck speechless for a moment.

Natasha flashed him a quick smile. "Ari, I really hope you enjoyed your brief stay, but I'm sure you're very anxious to get back to your family." Her eyes traveled down to his left hand. "I look forward to hearing from your father."

Ari inhaled her intoxicating fragrance, savoring the light floral scent. "You have a good day, Miss LeBlanc." He thought he detected a flicker of interest in her intense, warm brown eyes, but it was gone in a flash.

After she was gone, he went into the guest bedroom to grab his overnight tote. Just as he entered the master bedroom to retrieve his father's garment bag, a woman wearing a maid's uniform walked in.

"Oh, I'm so sorry," she said, looking panicked.

Ari smiled. "You're fine. I just came in to get this."

When he returned to the conference room, Ira and Malcolm had finished their discussion. Ira was putting documents into his attaché case.

Franklin appeared in the doorway to announce, "The limo is waiting downstairs to take you to the plane. I wish you a safe journey."

Ari and his father said their goodbyes to Ricardo and to Franklin.

They took the elevator down with Ira.

"Dad, I really don't think you should sell the hotel properties," Ari said when they were on their way to the airport. "We are more than capable of successfully managing the chain, despite what Natasha LeBlanc believes."

"When we get home, we will sit down with the rest of the family to examine *all* of our options, son. We will make this decision together — the same we have always done."

Pleased, Ari closed his eyes and settled back against the lush leather seats in the back of the limo. He wished he had seen more of Los Angeles, but there was time. He would be back.

Natasha LeBlanc would just have to accept that he was now a part of her world.

"Mr. Chase, these are the primary areas found to be in need of attention," Natasha began. "Inefficient service provided by undertrained and insufficient numbers of staff, poor levels of communication between management and ground staff, standard rooms and suites needing work, and the sports facilities were often unavailable due to an outdated booking system. However, on the positive side, this hotel had excellent food and a loyal sector of repeat customers aged sixty-plus."

"We have a new employee training program in place, and, of course, retraining will be done by all of the employees," said Mr. Chase.

"This is a good investment for you, but in order to maximize your dollars, you are going to need to upgrade your rooms — this will increase occupancy." Natasha paused a moment before continuing. "Mr. Chase, without substantial investment, it is often possible to improve the quality of service just through better staff training and communication skills. Little touches that make a world of difference can be missing."

She was so glad the meeting had finished on time. Natasha's day was a busy one, but she was grateful because she needed the money. She had two more appointments before having lunch with a potential client.

Natasha checked her watch. Ari and his father were on the plane by now. The flight was scheduled to depart in the next twenty minutes or so.

Her next two meetings were productive.

Natasha was grateful her day seemed to be going well. She left her office and got into her car. She was meeting with the CEO of the Savoy Hotel Group. While driving, Natasha rehearsed her presentation in her head.

Paul Pritzkin was just arriving when she got out of her car. They walked into the restaurant together.

They were seated immediately.

"I'm so glad you could meet with me at this late notice," Paul told her. "I have to leave this evening for London, and I won't be back for a couple of weeks."

"Thank you for calling me," she said. "I welcome the opportunity to work with your company."

They made small talk until their food arrived.

Natasha sliced into her entrée. "LeBlanc Consulting experts will help you outperform your local competition, Mr. Pritzkin. We specialize in hotel consulting. Within this small market niche, we offer a complete portfolio of services for the hospitality industry. You can combine the following services or products in order to obtain a package tailored to your specific needs."

Paul glanced down at the information she had given him. "You also specialize in operator selection?"

"Yes," Natasha responded. "If you are looking for a hotel group to run a planned or existing hotel, we can assist you with the selection of a suitable operator. We can also advise you with regard to the financial and legal aspects of a management or lease contract."

Two hours later, Natasha walked out of the restaurant with a check and signed contract. She hummed softly as she made her way to her car.

Natasha drove back to her office, grateful for the new clients she'd picked up today. She was responsible for twelve employees, and the new clients would help with overhead and payroll costs.

Her assistant had left a copy of *Hospitality News* in her office. On the cover was an article about Robert DePaul's death and his secret son. The media was predicting an all-out war between the DePaul family and Malcolm Alexander.

For Malcolm's sake, she prayed it wouldn't come to that. He seemed like a really nice man. As for Ari . . . the truth was that she liked Ari, although Natasha was pretty sure he didn't care much for her.

I probably would've tried harder to win him over if he weren't married. The thought made her laugh. Despite his marital status, she found him compelling, his magnetism potent.

How could I be attracted to this man? Natasha kept repeating *he's married* over and over in her head, but it was as if her heart refused to listen. She turned on the television to take her mind off Ari Alexander.

Natasha watched TV for about an hour before calling it a night. Her sister's engagement dinner was tomorrow night, so she and Joshua would be leaving first thing Saturday morning. Natasha was looking forward to seeing her family. She really didn't have anyone she was close to in Los Angeles, so she relished the time spent with her brother or sister.

After a relaxing shower, she slipped into her favorite sleepwear, a Lakers basketball jersey with Kobe Bryant's number. Natasha was a devoted basketball fan.

Ari drifted into her mind once more, causing her to toss a pillow at the wall in frustration. "Why can't I stop thinking about you?" she whispered. Natasha didn't want to think about Ari. He was married, and she respected the boundaries. Her ex-husband had never been faithful. She would never cross that line with a married man.

She wasn't that type of woman.

CHAPTER 5

Natasha and Joshua left early Saturday morning, heading to Phoenix for her sister's engagement dinner.

"I was about to get worried," her mother told her when they arrived shortly after twelve noon. "I thought you would be here an hour ago."

"There was a bad accident on the I-10." Natasha hugged her mother. "It's so good to see you."

Joshua hugged his grandmother next. "Where's Pop?" he asked, referring to his grandfather.

"He's in the backyard grilling some hot dogs."

Joshua's face lit up. "He is?"

Natasha met her mother's amused gaze and broke into a grin. Her son loved hot dogs, especially grilled hot dogs. "Put your cap on, Joshua."

The little boy did as he was told then ran

off to the back of the house.

"He looks good," her mother said.

Natasha agreed. "Joshua still tires pretty easily, but he's much better than before." She noted a look of sadness on her mother's face. "The doctor says that he's a little miracle. Joshua is going to be fine, Mama."

Corrine Henry had aged some with worry for her grandson — Natasha could see it on her mother's face. "He's fine," she repeated.

They were interrupted by the arrival of her brother, Nathan, and his family.

Natasha was enveloped into a tight bear hug. She laughed and then said, "Boy, you play too much."

She greeted her sister-in-law with a kiss on the cheek. "Kate, how do you put up with him?"

"My baby loves me," Nathan responded, wrapping an arm around his wife.

Natasha smiled at the look of happiness on her brother's face. "Yeah, she does love you. That makes me very happy."

He embraced her. "You know that I want the same for you."

She kissed his cheek. "I'm going to check on the children."

Joshua was in the backyard with his cousins, eating. Her father was sitting at the picnic table with them, talking. He was probably telling them stories of his days as a marine.

Natasha's eyes traveled the property that ran two acres long. A huge tent had been secured for Natalie's engagement dinner later that evening. A florist had arrived a few minutes ago with a van loaded with gorgeous arrangements.

Smiling, Natasha walked up to her father. "Hey, Daddy."

Nathan Sr. stood up and gave her a hug. "Hey, baby girl. How was the drive?"

"It was good," she responded. "Joshua slept most of the drive down. When he woke up, we sang songs the rest of the way here."

She stepped out of the way of the workers carrying centerpieces. "The flowers are lovely."

"I know they cost a lot of money," her father complained. "This is just the engagement party. I don't know if my wallet can survive the wedding."

Natasha laughed. "It won't be too bad, Daddy. You know Natalie — she's the sensible one."

"I also know your mother." He winked at her.

"I know you're over there talking about me," Corrine said, walking toward them. "Your father complaining about that wallet of his again?"

Natasha and her father both cracked up with laughter.

"I need to unpack our clothes for the dinner tonight," she told her parents. "I'll be back in a few. Dad, please don't let Joshua have another hot dog."

"I'm not going to let the boy starve, Natasha. If he's hungry, let him eat."

"Just give him some fruit . . . please. I'm trying to get him to eat more fruit."

After eliciting a promise from her father, Natasha headed back inside the house.

Nathan had carried her luggage into the house and to her old bedroom, so all Natasha had to do now was unpack. They were going to be in Phoenix for only one night, so they didn't bring much.

She hung up her dress and laid out the suit Joshua would be wearing for the dinner this evening.

Natasha freshened up before joining her mother in the kitchen. "What can I do to help?" she asked.

Corrine glanced around the huge gourmet kitchen. "Everything has been taken care of, sweetheart. Mandy and Alice will be here in a couple of hours to get everything set up for dinner."

Her mother owned a catering company,

and her employees would be serving the guests this evening.

Natasha's eyes bounced around, taking in the attractive display of desserts for the dinner, the party favors and the appetizers. "I can't have any of this stuff, Mama. Just looking at it makes me gain weight," she teased. "Everything looks really nice, Mama. You always do a wonderful job." Natasha recalled the great selection of food at her wedding celebration, and how beautiful the church and reception had been decorated. Everything had been perfect, except the marriage.

"I've been hearing a lot about Robert DePaul's son," her mother said.

Natasha nodded. "I hate to say this, but if his son had been Caucasian, I don't think there would be all of this fuss."

Corrine shrugged. "I don't know, Natasha. A secret son is a secret son — people love to hear about the skeletons of others coming out of the closet."

Natasha grabbed an apple and took a bite. "I've met Malcolm Alexander. He's actually a very nice man."

"So do you think it's true? Is he really Robert DePaul's son?"

"I don't believe Robert would've left his entire estate to Malcolm if he wasn't sure,"

Natasha said. "He wasn't out of his mind like the media is trying to portray. I think Robert just wanted to do right by his only son." She shook her head. "It's crazy what they are accusing him of — Malcolm didn't know anything about Robert being his father."

Corrine picked up an apple and bit into it. "So what is this Malcolm Alexander like?"

"He's very Southern," Natasha said with a smile. "A true Southern gentleman. He's quiet. I can tell that he thinks before he speaks. Now his son . . . Ari is the opposite of his father. He's never met an opinion he didn't share."

"Sounds like you two have had some fireworks."

"We have," Natasha admitted. "But it's because he's extremely protective of his father."

"Is he handsome?"

Natasha smiled. "When Ari's not scowling at me, he looks pretty good. Before you start trying to match us up — you can forget about it. He's married."

"Are you sure?"

"He wears a wedding ring, Mom," Natasha responded with a chuckle. "He's as married as they come."

"That's too bad," her mother responded.

"Well, Malcolm Alexander does have other sons, right?"

"Why are you always trying to find a man for me? Mom, I don't have time for romance. I have my son to worry about."

Corrine's mouth curved with tenderness. "Natasha, you're still young — you should enjoy your life."

"My life is fine, Mom," she insisted. "Really, it is."

Her mother didn't look as if she believed her, so Natasha decided to let the matter drop. Her marriage lasted all of one year. Her husband ran off with a stripper shortly after he found out she was pregnant. It wasn't until he was gone that she found out about all the other women he had been seeing — some before they were married. Calvin didn't want to pay child support, so he voluntarily terminated his parental rights.

Natasha had finally made peace with the past, and she desired to just move forward with her life. Her beautiful son had come out of the marriage; he was the only pleasant thing about her relationship with her ex-husband, the serial cheater.

Saturday afternoon, Ari and his siblings joined their parents at the dining-room table.

Malcolm and Barbara had called a family meeting. Even their two youngest children, who were attending college in Atlanta, had come home for the weekend.

"We're all here and accounted for," Kellen said with a chuckle.

Barbara smiled. "Seems like the only time we see you is when there's a family meeting, son."

He gave a slight shrug. "Mom, you know me. I have places to go and people to see."

She gave him a playful pinch. "Ask those people for money next month when your rent has to be paid."

"How about you come to Atlanta?" Kellen inquired. "We can do a mother-son dinner or something."

"Let's get started," Malcolm interjected. He gave them a brief recap of what had transpired during their trip to Beverly Hills. "So where we are now is that there's an offer on the table to buy the hotel properties. We suspect it's DePaul's relatives."

"Why are they being so sneaky about it?" Zaire asked.

"I don't care why," Ari responded. "Dad, I don't think we should entertain any offers to buy the hotel properties. I know we're talking about a chain of luxury resorts — the hard work has already been done for us.

All we have to do is maintain the high standards set forth by Robert DePaul. Family, we can do this."

Blaze nodded in agreement. "I'm with Ari on this. It's not like we have to reinvent the wheel."

Sage nodded in agreement. "Dad, I agree with Ari and Blaze."

Malcolm looked in Drayden's direction. "I'd like to hear your thoughts on this, too."

"Dad, this is something you and Mom have dreamed about. I think you should do it. We can sell the hotels here in Georgia or do some major renovations so that it will reflect the same luxury as the DePaul properties. It could be one of the few DePaul hotels on the East Coast."

Ari nodded in agreement. "I like that idea."

"You all really want this?" Malcolm inquired, looking around the table at his children.

They all nodded.

He turned to face his wife. "What do you think about all this, hon?"

Barbara smiled. "Malcolm, I agree with our children. This *is* something we've always dreamed about."

"If we keep the hotels, then I would prefer that we do this as a family," Malcolm said.

"I'm in," Ari announced.

"Me, too," Sage and Blaze said in unison.

"Dad, I'm in for moving to Los Angeles," Drayden said. "But you know I want to open my own accounting firm."

"So does this mean you'll be moving to California and starting your business there?" Barbara asked.

"Yes, ma'am. I believe I'd be more successful out there than here in Aspen."

The two younger siblings, Zaire and Kellen, were quiet.

Malcolm met his youngest daughter's gaze. "What are you thinking about, Zaire? I'm not used to you being so quiet."

There were chuckles around the table.

"Forget y'all," Zaire muttered. "Dad, I've just been sitting here listening to everybody. There is something none of you have considered."

"What's that, dear?" Barbara asked.

"Do you really think the rest of Robert DePaul's family will let us walk in and just take over the estate? I don't think they are going to give up that easily."

"She does have a point," Kellen interjected. "Everything sounds all nice, but it's not going to be an easy road. I don't think we should get our hopes up. I know DePaul left everything to you, Dad, but his estate could be tied up in court for years. Do we really want to put ourselves through that?"

"The will is ironclad," Ari told his brother. "The law is on our side. Robert DePaul made sure of that before he died. If his family takes us to court, they lose their share of the inheritance."

"Hey, I just wanted to throw that out there," Kellen said. "Leona Helmsley left twelve million dollars to her dog, Trouble, and the courts reduced it to two million. You know that I don't mind a good fight, but there's no point in getting all scuffed up in a battle we can't win."

"That was because the Queen of Mean was declared mentally unfit when she made her will." Ari stated. "Robert DePaul was of sound mind when he died."

Zaire glanced at her father. "We're all on board, Dad. Your DePaul relatives won't know what hit them when the Alexander family arrives in Beverly Hills."

Natasha strolled about, nodding at a few people as she moved about in the enclosed tent. She made her way over to where Natalie was standing with her fiancé.

"Where's the munchkin?" her sister asked.

"With Dad," Natasha responded with a

chuckle. "They wanted some male-bonding time."

"How is he feeling?" Natalie inquired.

"He was a little tired after the trip, but he's so excited to see everyone." Natasha glanced around. "Where is Nathan?" she asked.

Natalie surveyed the room. "Our brother is probably somewhere making out with his wife," her sister responded with a chuckle. "Guess we'll be meeting another niece or nephew in nine months."

Natasha shook her head. "They have a set of twins. We're triplets . . . they just might end up with quads or something scarier."

Natalie and her fiancé laughed.

"Don't laugh," Natasha warned. "You two haven't gotten started yet."

Ten minutes later, everyone was seated at tables dining on garlic-lime chicken, grilled asparagus with lime dressing, four-cheese mashed potatoes with wild mushrooms, and onion bread.

"Mama outdid herself with this menu," Natalie whispered to her.

Natasha agreed. She sliced off a piece of the tender chicken and stuck it into her mouth, savoring the flavor.

She couldn't help but notice how Natalie was glowing with happiness. Natasha was genuinely happy for her sister, but it also reminded her of how lonely she felt without a man in her life. Having the support of someone special would help ease some of the tension of what her son had to go through.

After the entrée and before dessert was served, her father stood up to make a toast. Natasha excused herself and went to check on Joshua. He was seated at the children's table with his cousins. She found them laughing and teasing each other.

She turned to walk away, spotted her brother standing a few yards away and went to join him. "What have you been up to?" Natasha asked as she straightened his tie.

He grinned. "Do you really want to know?"

Shaking her head, Natasha asked, "Don't you and Kate ever get tired of each other?"

"No, we don't," Nathan responded. His expression grew serious when he said, "I never thought I'd ever love anyone as much as I love her."

"That's really wonderful," she murmured. "My sister-in-law is a lucky woman."

He hugged her. "There is a man out there somewhere looking for you, Natasha. He's going to find you one day soon. You just

make sure that you're ready for Mr. Wonderful."

"I'm not sure I'll know him when I see
him," she confessed. "I thought I'd met my
Mr. Right when I married Calvin."

Nathan frowned. "That dude didn't deserve you or Joshua."

His words touched her deeply. "Thanks,
Nathan."

"Hey, this is what big brothers are for."

Natasha slapped his arm. "You are only
ten minutes older than me."

"That still makes me the oldest."

She laughed. "Only in your world."

The music started, and Joshua rushed
over to her. "Mommy, would you like to
dance?"

"Sure, sweetie."

Joshua led her to the dance floor.

They danced to one song then Natalie approached them, saying, "Okay, munchkin,
it's my turn to dance with you."

She kissed the top of Joshua's head then
whispered, "Don't overdo it, okay?"

He nodded and then started moving to
the beat of the music.

"Are you up to dancing with your old
dad?"

Natasha turned around to find her father
standing there. "I would be honored,

Daddy."

I have the most wonderful family in the world, she thought to herself.

That evening when they returned to her parents' house, Natasha helped Joshua get into his pajamas.

"Mommy, I can do it," he fussed.

"Okay," she said, hiding hurt feelings. "I was only trying to help you."

Joshua looked up at her and said, "I love you, but Mommy, you gotta let me do it. I'm a big boy."

"He's right," her father said from the doorway.

Natasha walked over to her father and said, "He's such a sweetheart. I can't imagine what my life was like before he came into it."

Nathan Sr. took her by the hand and led her down the hall. "Honey, I know that sometimes you get scared, and that's okay, but I want you to know that you don't have to go through this alone. Your mother and I will come to Los Angeles and we'll stay as long as you need us."

Natasha shook her head. "You don't have to do that. We're fine. The leukemia is in remission and his doctors are great."

Her father looked concerned. "How are you paying for all this?"

"Insurance covered some," she responded. "Robert left me some money, so stop worrying. We're fine."

"Would you tell me if you weren't?" he asked.

"Yes, Daddy," Natasha lied. "I would." Her father had heart problems, and the last thing she wanted was to have him stressed and worried about her and Joshua.

CHAPTER 6

Barbara had breakfast on the table when Ari and his siblings came downstairs Sunday morning.

"I thought I smelled bacon," Kellen said. "I've missed your cooking, Mama. Zaire needs to spend more time with you, especially in the kitchen, because she can't cook tap water."

"I'm not your woman or your maid," his sister snapped. "I'm your sister. Why don't you learn your way around a kitchen?"

Ari laughed at the expression on Kellen's face. "What's wrong with you, man?" he asked his brother. "You need to learn how to cook something, or stock up on some peanut butter and jelly."

"Hey, Mama, if you and Dad don't need the chef, can I have him?" Kellen inquired. "I'm just saying. Cooking is not my thing, you know."

Sage brushed by her youngest brother.

"Kellen, you're a big boy. Learn to cook. Ari, Blaze and Drayden can all cook. You ought to be embarrassed."

"He's spoiled," Zaire stated.

"And you're not," Kellen retorted.

Zaire sent a sharp glance in his direction. "We are not talking about me."

Malcolm entered the dining room. "No matter how old you all get, the arguments never change."

They all settled down at the table.

Blaze blessed the food.

Ari passed the bowl of hash browns to Drayden. "Pass the eggs, please."

Sage did as he requested.

He spooned some on his plate and then passed them to Kellen. Ari recalled how much his late wife enjoyed the Alexander family meals. She didn't come from a close family, so April relished spending time with her close-knit in-laws.

When Drayden mentioned dating, Ari's mind traveled to Natasha. Since meeting her, Natasha seemed to always take control of his thoughts. He couldn't deny that there was an invisible thread of magnetism that was drawing them together.

The DNA results would be back in a couple of days, and Ari and his father were planning to fly back to Los Angeles at the end of the week. This would give him some time to get his emotions in order.

"Eat up," Malcolm told everyone. "We have to leave for church in about an hour."

Two hours after she and Joshua returned to Los Angeles, Harold called, wanting to meet with her.

"I just got back from Phoenix and I'm exhausted," Natasha told him. "Besides, there is no one here to watch my son." All she wanted to do was relax for the rest of the evening with Joshua.

"Do you mind if I come over?" Harold inquired. "I'll even bring dinner."

"Sure. I'll see you within the hour." She groaned softly after she hung up the phone. Natasha really wasn't in the mood for company, but she knew that Harold would never take no for an answer. He wanted to discuss Malcolm and the inheritance — it was all he seemed to focus on since Robert's death. Natasha didn't recall any show of grief on Harold's face over the loss of his uncle.

People grieved in different ways, she rationalized.

The doorbell rang.

Natasha glanced over at the clock on the wall. Harold was early.

"Mommy, are we having company?" Joshua asked.

"Mr. Harold wanted to come over and visit with us." She prayed he would keep himself in check. Natasha didn't want anyone upsetting Joshua.

"Oh," her son said and then returned his attention to the television.

She ran her fingers through her hair before opening the front door.

"I know I'm early," he said. "I didn't want the food to get cold." Holding up a large bag, he added, "I brought Italian."

He knew it was her favorite.

Natasha stepped out of the way so that he could enter the condo. She led him to the dining room, where they arranged the various containers of food on the table.

"What didn't you bring?" Natasha asked, looking at all of the selections. There was garlic bread, spaghetti with meatballs, fettuccini with a pesto sauce, penne rustico and chicken marsala. Harold had even brought dessert, an Italian cream cake.

"I didn't know what you had a taste for, so I ordered all of your favorites."

She awarded him a smile. "I must admit that I'm really surprised you would remember something like this."

Joshua ran into the dining room. "I want

some spaghetti, please." He looked up at Harold and said, "Hey . . ."

"How are you feeling, buddy?" Harold asked.

"Fine," Joshua responded as he took a seat at the table.

"That's fine, sweetie," Natasha said.

Harold eyed her son. "He's a handsome little boy, Natasha."

"I certainly think so," she responded. "Thank you for all you've done, Harold. I appreciate it."

Harold held the chair out for Natasha then sat down across from her. Natasha prepared a plate for her son then one for Harold.

"You're spoiling me," he said.

"I'm just being a good hostess," Natasha told him.

She fixed a plate for herself, choosing to sample the penne rustico and the chicken marsala.

They kept the conversation neutral while they ate.

"Thanks for dinner," Natasha said when they finished. "Everything was delicious."

Harold helped her put away the rest of the food while Joshua returned to the den to watch television.

"So what do you think Malcolm will

decide?" Harold asked as he leaned against the counter in the kitchen.

"I don't know," she responded. "He's not an easy man to read."

"What about the son?"

Natasha peered at Harold. "Ari is a lot like his father. However, he has made it pretty clear that he thinks his father should keep the hotels."

They ventured into the living room to talk.

Harold sat down on the sofa beside Natasha, saying, "I still don't understand how Uncle Robert could so something like this to our family. Those hotels should have remained with us — his family. If he wanted to give something to Malcolm, why didn't he just send him a check?"

"Harold, the answer to that is pretty clear, don't you think? He wanted to do right by his only son."

"The DNA results aren't in," Harold uttered in response. "Until then, I won't acknowledge him as my uncle's son."

"Robert recognized him as his son," Natasha stated. "The results will be in by Tuesday, but in the eyes of the law, this is all that matters."

Angry, Harold glared at her.

Natasha shrugged. "You may not want to hear the truth, but there's no escaping it,

Harold."

He leaned forward in his chair. "There's something I've always wanted to ask you."

"What?"

"Were you ever involved with my uncle?"

"No," she uttered. "Robert DePaul was a mentor to me. *Nothing more.*"

"Hey, I just wondered, given his penchant for chocolate."

Natasha resisted the urge to throw hot water into his face. "You are so despicable at times."

"Hey, I do understand. For a while there we —"

She shook her head. "Don't go there, Harold. You were the one who couldn't handle being seen with a black woman on your arm. You don't mind when it's behind closed doors, but out in the open . . ."

She glimpsed a flash of anger in his eyes.

"I have a lot of respect for you, Natasha, but I have to warn you. Don't push me. I truly cared for her."

"You broke her heart." Harold was involved with her roommate, Trudy, when they were in college. "When people suspected you were dating her — actually, when your friends started to question you — that's when you dumped her. She was in love with you."

The air was pregnant with tense silence for a moment.

"Do you ever hear from her?"

Natasha nodded.

"How is she?"

"What do you care, Harold?"

He opened his checkbook and began writing. "I trust you will do your best to convince Malcolm Alexander to sell the hotel properties. I can't wait for this wave of humiliation to be over. We haven't even been allowed to grieve for my uncle in peace."

"Why does this bother you so much?" she questioned. "Is this about race?"

"No," Harold responded forcefully. "I have been like a son to Uncle Robert. He used to tell me that I was like a son to him. He knew how much I loved the hotels . . . he knew, but he leaves them to someone he thinks is his child. I'm sorry, but it just doesn't make sense."

"It made perfect sense to your uncle, Harold."

"Whose side are you on, Natasha?"

"Harold, I am helping you," she pointed out. "But I am not going to lie about your uncle's state of mind during his illness. His last wishes were very clear."

"Natasha, all I want is what should have

been mine from the beginning. The hotels should be mine. Actually, the entire estate should have been left to me. I was the one who never abandoned Uncle Robert. I was by his side when he died."

"So you think he shouldn't have left anything for his son?"

"I didn't say that, Natasha. My uncle was always feeling sorry for those less fortunate. He gave away so much money . . ."

"He was a very generous man, Harold. I admired that about him."

"Yet all he left you was a mere ten thousand dollars and the deed to your office building."

"He didn't have to do that," Natasha countered. "I'm very grateful to Robert."

Harold chuckled. "Look at you. You are always loyal to the very end."

Natasha chose not to respond.

He rose to his feet. "As soon as you hear from Malcolm Alexander, I trust you will let me know."

"This is the agreement we have," she responded. "I'm not dense, Harold. You don't have to beat me over the head with this. The ball is in Malcolm's court at this point."

"It's up to you to persuade him to our way of thinking," he insisted.

Natasha's mood veered sharply to anger. "Thanks again for dinner, Harold, but I'm feeling really tired."

"Kicking me out?" he asked.

Natasha folded her arms across her chest. "I don't mean to be rude, Harold. I'm just tired."

"I understand." He made his way to the door. "Your son is looking well. I pray that he stays that way."

"Goodbye, Harold." She threw the words at him like stones.

When he was gone, Natasha released a long sigh of relief. She had known Harold for a very long time, but there was something about him that bothered her. There were times he seemed racist, but then there was his relationship with her former roommate. But like Robert, he worried too much about what his family thought of him. He was more like a puppet.

One of the things she admired about Ari was that he was comfortable in his own skin. He respected Malcolm but wasn't afraid to disagree with him. It's too bad he was already taken, she thought sadly. Lately, it seemed good men usually were either dead or married.

The telephone rang, and Ari answered it,

since he was the only one close by.

"Ari?" the voice said on the other end. "It's Natasha. I was calling to speak to your father."

Her voice was a velvet murmur.

Ari felt his heart race, and he swallowed hard. "Hello, Natasha."

"I'm sorry — did I call the wrong number?" she asked. "I thought I was calling your father."

"No, it's the right number. We're all here with my parents this weekend," he explained. "Mom and Dad just left for their walk. They should be back in about thirty minutes."

"Oh," she murmured.

"Did you need something?" he asked, not wanting to end the call.

"No, Ari, I just wanted to check in with your father. Just in case he had some questions. If he does, he can call me back."

"I'll tell him that you called," Ari told her. "Don't tell me that you work on your days off. You should be out enjoying the California sunshine."

"How is the weather in Georgia?" she inquired. "It's been raining all day here."

"Nice," he responded. "Humid, though."

They sat on the phone for a brief moment in silence.

"I don't want to keep you from your family, Ari. Enjoy the rest of your day."

"Do you want my dad to call you back?"

"It can wait until tomorrow. I don't want to disrupt your family gathering."

"Are you sure?"

"Yes, I'm sure."

His voice cut the silence. "Well, I'm about to beat up on my brothers in basketball. Don't work too hard, Miss LeBlanc. Have some fun."

"Is that your way of telling me that you have skills?"

Ari laughed. "I'm just saying."

"I'd like to hear how that game really turns out," she remarked.

"Hey, I can play some ball. I'm not bragging, though — I'm just saying."

Natasha chuckled. "I'm not bragging either, but I have b-ball skills, too."

Her words surprised him. "Really?"

"I attended college on an athletic scholarship," Natasha responded matter-of-factly.

"I'm impressed."

"Don't be until you see me out on the court."

Ari chuckled. "I'm going to have to check you out."

"I don't play as much as I used to," she told him. "I was in an adult league, but I have a lot going on in my life right now."

"It was nice talking to you, Natasha. I'll let my dad know that you called."

They ended the call.

Ari turned to find his sister Zaire standing there, her arms folded across her chest and a scowl on her face. "I thought she was the enemy."

He gave a short laugh. "I wouldn't exactly call her the enemy, Zaire."

"If she's not with us, then she has to be against us." Her voice was cold and exact. "You better watch yourself around that woman, Ari."

"I'll take that under advisement." He followed her outside.

"I can't believe you're in here talking about playing basketball," Zaire grumbled. "The only sport she's playing is *you.*"

Her words gave Ari pause. It was true that he didn't trust Natasha, but would she try to get to his father through him?

CHAPTER 7

Ari, Blaze and Drayden met their father for lunch on Monday. Malcolm wanted to speak with his sons alone.

"What time do you get off work, Ari?" Blaze inquired. "I'm going to the gym this evening."

"I can meet you there at six," he said.

Malcolm joined them a few minutes later. "Sorry I'm late. I had a last-minute phone call."

A waitress appeared at the table almost immediately to take their drink orders.

While waiting for her to return, they decided on what they wanted to eat. Sandals Steak House was located inside the Alexander Hotel. Ari and his family knew every selection, so they didn't bother looking at the menu.

The waitress returned with a tray of drinks. She took their food orders before walking away from the table a second time.

Ari finished off a glass of water before saying, "Dad, I'm glad you decided not to sell."

"Some of the executive team members are related to Robert DePaul," Malcolm said. "We have to be aware that we really don't know how much of the staff will be loyal to that family."

"Well, the first thing you should do is put a new managing director in place," Blaze suggested. "I believe that person should be Ari. He's been in the position of general manager at our hotel for five years. He's more than qualified. I also have a feeling that Robert's relatives are all going to jump ship rather than work for you. We need to be prepared for that."

"I agree," Drayden said. "If Ari is going to be the new managing director, then he will need to move to Los Angeles as soon as possible. It's key for him to orient the staff or hire new staff so that they completely understand your expectations, policies and procedures."

"Drayden's right," Ari responded. "We need to transition quickly and smoothly."

"Sage told me that she wants to take charge of the residential properties," Malcolm said.

"She is a real estate agent, and she's done quite well for herself," Blaze commented.

"This is what she's wanted to do for a while. Sage was looking to move to a bigger city where she could broker high-end homes."

"Blaze, are you interested in joining the family business?" Ari questioned.

"Actually, I am," Blaze replied. "How about a VP of sales position? I've been director of sales and marketing with Hanson's Grocery chain for almost six years now. I'd like to do something a little more challenging."

Malcolm made notes as they talked. "Ari, would you consider moving out to Los Angeles right away? If we do this, then I'm going to need someone I can trust to be my eyes and ears until your mother and I can get things straight out here. We'll join you in a couple of months permanently. In the meantime, I will be flying back and forth."

Ari was touched by his father's faith in him. "I'll do whatever you need, Dad."

"Blaze, if you're serious, then you should start transitioning out of Hanson's," Malcolm said.

"I'll give them thirty-days' notice," said Blaze, "so that they have time to find a suitable replacement."

Ari glanced over at Drayden. "Have you given any more thought to moving to California?"

His brother nodded. "I've been researching office buildings in Los Angeles. I think I'd like to work somewhere on Wilshire Boulevard."

Drayden's words made Ari smile. He was thrilled that the entire family would be relocating to California. His younger siblings had already planned to join them after they graduated from grad school.

"I'm glad we're all going to be together," Blaze said.

"If this hadn't come up, I was considering relocating to Atlanta or Charlotte," Drayden confessed. "I love Aspen, but for business . . . it just wasn't going to work out."

Their food arrived.

Malcolm gave thanks for their lunch and for the gift from Robert.

Ari eyed his father. "Dad, you're not just doing this because we want you to — this is something you and Mom want, as well, right?"

"I admit that I had no intentions of accepting the inheritance. I had planned to turn it over to Robert's other relatives, but your mother gave me a different perspective of the situation. She reminded me that Robert had been tracking me, and she believes he truly felt I was the right choice as his heir — his successor. She doesn't doubt his love for me, but Robert DePaul has always been an astute businessman. This wasn't just about me being his son. It was a business decision, pure and simple."

Ari smiled. "Mom is a smart businesswoman in her own right."

Malcolm agreed. "She appointed herself as hospitality director. She made me think it was my idea, however."

They all laughed.

Blaze wiped his mouth on the edge of his napkin. "Robert made the right decision, Dad. We have to remember that there are things we don't know about the rest of his family, but apparently Robert knew all of their secrets. Maybe there is a reason why he did what he did."

"He wanted to acknowledge his son," Drayden contributed. "I don't know why we are trying to overanalyze this."

Ari couldn't help but wonder if there was something more behind Robert's generosity. Why wouldn't he leave his estate to his nephew — the one who had been by his side for years?

"You haven't heard anything from Ira or Malcolm?" Harold asked.

Natasha held her temper in check. "I told you twice that I haven't heard a word," she retorted tartly. She was irritated to find him sitting in her office. She vowed to have a serious talk with her assistant.

"I wonder what they're plotting."

"Why do you think they're plotting?" Natasha asked. "Malcolm already has the inheritance — what more could he gain?"

Agitated, Harold began pacing back and forth across the floor. "I'm sure he's smart enough to know that we will fight him tooth and nail. He has to know that we will challenge the will."

"Are you sure you want to do that, Harold?"

He stared at her. "Why not? What do I have to lose?"

"Your share of the estate," Natasha said. "The will was very clear."

Harold muttered a curse.

"If you want my advice — just wait and see what Malcolm decides before you work yourself up into a stroke or heart attack."

"What he needs to do is stay in that country town with the Alexander Hotel," Harold said tersely. "That's where he belongs."

"Harold, let's get one thing clear," Natasha demanded. "I agreed with your plan only because I feel that Malcolm doesn't have enough experience in running the company. If I felt otherwise, I wouldn't have gone along with this."

"You make me question your loyalty when you say things like that," Harold responded. "Can I trust you, Natasha?"

"Have I ever exposed any of your secrets, Harold?"

"I hate all of this tension between us."

"It's not my doing." Natasha checked her watch. "I have an appointment in about twenty minutes."

"I've grown to care for you over the years. I was thinking we could go to Catalina Island for the Memorial Day weekend. We —"

She interrupted him by saying, "Harold, don't . . ."

"I think we would be good together."

"How is it that you keep forgetting that you have a wife?" Natasha questioned. "I'm sure Sara isn't interested in sharing her husband with another woman. But not only that — I know you, Harold."

"You know, you're always accusing me of being a racist," he said in a nasty tone. "I think you should look in the mirror." Harold stood up and walked to the door. "I'll be in touch."

Natasha shook her head in disbelief.

The DNA test results proved without a doubt that Robert had indeed fathered Malcolm, just as Ari didn't doubt they would.

After receiving the results, his father made arrangements for them to travel to Los Angeles. The plane was already en route to Atlanta. Ari and his father would be leaving first thing on Thursday morning.

Ari was looking forward to starting over in Los Angeles. Malcolm would be returning home, but he would be staying. Malcolm wanted to hire someone to replace Ari as managing director. His parents planned to join Ari in a couple of months. In the meantime, Malcolm would be flying back and forth.

The day merged into night.

Ari went to bed around midnight but was up before his alarm clock went off. He got up and spent some time reflecting on his life and all that he was leaving behind. He was going to sell the house he had shared with April and donate all of the furnishings. He had been undecided about his Land Rover until now. He was going to have it transported to Los Angeles.

Drayden drove Ari and their father to the airport.

When they hit some traffic on I-20, Ari said, "Feels good not to have to worry about missing a flight again."

Drayden chuckled. "I've never flown first-class, but I have a feeling it doesn't compare to having a family plane."

Ari agreed. "Wait until you get on it, Drayden. You will never fly commercial again."

"Or coach," Malcolm interjected.

Forty-five minutes later, they were on the plane. They wouldn't land for another five hours.

Ari and Malcolm spent the entire flight poring over information on the hotel properties. Ari intended to hit the ground running. They couldn't afford to waste any time, but the most urgent item on their list was removing Harold from his position as managing director.

Malcolm was still sifting through paperwork regarding all of Robert's assets. He and Ira had spoken almost every day. Outside of the hotel chain, his father had discovered that he also owned two restaurants.

The smiling flight attendant brought them breakfast.

"Son, there's something you should know."

Reaching for his orange juice, Ari looked over at his father. "What is it?"

"The Nevada State Contractors Board has launched an investigation against Robert. It seems that two of the hotels in that state had renovations completed without obtaining the necessary building permits. We need to find out who signed off on that construction."

"I'll make that a priority," Ari responded.

"If we are at fault, then we will need to settle this as quietly as possible. I don't want news of this getting out."

"Do you think it was Robert?"

Malcolm shrugged. "I don't know. He was ill for a while. It could've been an innocent oversight."

A limo was waiting for them when the plane landed. They were driven straight to the hotel in Beverly Hills. Natasha was in the lobby when he arrived.

"It's nice to see you again, Mr. Alexander," Natasha said as she shook his hand. "Good to see you, as well, Ari."

He returned her smile.

They gathered in the conference room.

Ira arrived fifteen minutes later.

As soon as everyone was seated, Malcolm

announced, "My family and I discussed the proposal at length and we've made a decision."

Natasha glanced over at Ari. She couldn't read Malcolm's expression, but she was trying to see if she could get an idea of where this was leading. Harold and the other DePaul relatives would be outraged if their plans fell through. She couldn't help but wonder what would happen to her son. They needed the money for his medical expenses.

"After a lot of thought and conversation with my family, we have decided not to sell the hotel properties."

Natasha cringed inwardly. Harold was going to be furious, but there was nothing she could do.

"I hope your clients won't be too disappointed," Ari said to her. "Give the DePaul family our regards."

Natasha was mildly surprised that they had figured out she was representing Harold and the rest of the DePaul family. It wasn't a real stretch to figure out that they would try to buy the properties to keep them in the family.

"I guess you should be on your way to break the news to the DePaul relatives."

Natasha boldly met Ari's gaze. "I hope you and your family know what you're getting into."

"We do," he responded.

She was aware that Malcolm and Ira both remained quiet. They sat there listening to the exchange between her and Ari.

"Why do you want this so badly?" Natasha asked.

"It's in our blood," Ari responded. "This much should be obvious to you."

She nodded in understanding. "Well, I wish you much success in this venture."

"Do you really?"

"Ari, I don't want to see your family fail — this is why I thought it was best that you sell the properties. Your family could've made millions of dollars from the sale alone."

"Do you think this is about money?" he asked. "We are not ruled by the mighty dollar."

"I didn't mean it that way."

"This is a dream of ours, as a family, Natasha. This is a legacy that we can leave for our children and their children. My parents are smart businesspeople. You don't have to worry about us. We are more than qualified to manage the DePaul properties. Robert knew this — he believed in my father."

115

The fire in his eyes displayed Ari's passion. He probably wanted this more than Malcolm.

"I assume you will also be coming on board," she said.

Ari shrugged. "If this is what my father wishes."

He's not about to reveal anything to me, she thought silently. She glanced over at Malcolm, who had been listening to their exchange, his expression a blank page.

"If there is anything I can do to make this transition a smooth one, please call me," she said.

Malcolm shifted his position in his chair. "I would like you to stay on for a year as a consultant, Miss LeBlanc. We also want the option to extend your services for another year after that. Ira can draw up the contract."

She stole a peek at Ari. He had not fully recovered from the shock. Apparently, Malcolm hadn't discussed this with his son.

Natasha returned her attention to Malcolm. "Thank you for the offer. I would be more than happy to stay on."

She could feel Ari's eyes on her.

Smiling, she looked at him and said, "Looks like we're going to be working together."

CHAPTER 8

Ari bristled at the news that Malcolm wanted to keep Natasha on board. It wasn't just that he didn't trust her. She stirred something in him that defied description, and he didn't want to be forced to work so closely with her.

However, he couldn't change his father's mind once he'd made a decision.

When he had the chance to get Malcolm alone, he said, "Dad, I'm not sure keeping Natasha on as consultant is a good idea. I don't think we can trust her."

"We can keep an eye on her if she's close by," his father responded. "I want to know every move this little lady makes — at least until we know the lay of the land."

Seeing Malcolm's point, Ari nodded in agreement.

Natasha walked back into the conference room. "Am I interrupting?"

Ari wondered how much of their conversation she had overheard, but her face was devoid of emotion. "Where is Ira?"

"He's finishing up a call," she responded. "He should be in here shortly."

Ari eyed her as she sat across from him making notes.

The attorney entered the room and closed the door.

"I might as well tell you that I intend to make a change in the name," Malcolm announced as Ira took his seat. "The hotels will now be known as the Alexander-DePaul Hotel & Spa Resorts in honor of both my fathers."

Surprised, Natasha turned her gaze to Ari, who said, "I think it's perfect."

"May I ask why you decided to change the name?" she asked.

Malcolm finished the last of his water. "The rebranding will unite all members of the organization with one shared vision for success. We believe this evolution honors our heritage and better positions us to move forward under a unified brand."

"I'll get all of the paperwork started," Ira stated.

Natasha didn't put up any argument against the name change, which surprised Ari. He had assumed she would be against rebranding.

"I would like to see the rest of this hotel," Malcolm said. He hadn't wanted to take any tours until he decided what he was going to do.

Ari and his father followed Natasha out of the penthouse and to the elevator.

"All of the properties are beautiful, but I have to admit that this one is my favorite," she was saying.

"It is a masterpiece," Ari commented. "I told my dad that it looks so much better in person."

She nodded. "The photographs are stunning, but to truly appreciate it, you have to see it."

"Outside of acquisition, disposition and development consulting, what other services does your company offer?" Ari asked her.

"We conduct appraisals and valuation, feasibility analysis and specialized research such as brand-repositioning studies."

"Where did you receive your MBA?"

She smiled. "Stanford. How about you? Where did you obtain yours?"

"University of Pennsylvania," he responded.

"The Wharton School of Business?"

He nodded.

"I'm impressed," Natasha murmured. "I'm not surprised, though. You seem like

Wharton alumni."

"Why do you say that?"

"I have a friend who went to Wharton, and you remind me of him."

"An old boyfriend?"

She shook her head no. "He was my best friend."

"Was?"

"He passed away three years ago," Natasha said. "He was killed by a drunk driver."

"I'm sorry to hear about that," Ari responded.

Natasha took them to see a couple of the empty rooms. She had the housekeeper unlock one on the eighth floor that had just been cleaned. "The guest rooms are spacious, ranging from five hundred to two thousand square feet," she told them. "All of the hotels offer more than a place to temporarily retreat in luxury. As you already know, there are a limited number of residences ranging from two to five bedrooms with ample room to accommodate housekeepers, personal assistants or nannies."

"Is there a private garage for residents?" Ari inquired.

Natasha nodded. "The residents have a personal valet. They can just drop their keys with the valet and take the private elevator up to the penthouse floors."

Malcolm and Ari met with the hotel management. Natasha introduced them as the new owners. His father answered a few questions but promised that more information would be released over the next few days.

"I can't help but wonder what they have been told," Ari said in a low voice.

"It doesn't matter, son," Malcolm responded. "We will set things straight."

Ari glanced over at Natasha. "I'd like to go to the corporate offices tomorrow morning."

She nodded. "Sure, no problem. I just have to check my calendar to make sure my day is clear."

"Actually, let's not wait until tomorrow. We can go later this afternoon. I might as well face off with Harold DePaul sooner than later."

"He's in New York," Natasha told him. "But he is scheduled to return sometime this evening."

"You know this because . . ."

"There are two private planes. The one your father is traveling on was Robert's private plane. The other is a company jet."

"Is he there on business?" Malcolm inquired.

"That, I don't know," she answered. "Mr. Alexander, are you planning on keeping Harold DePaul on board?"

"Maybe in some capacity," he responded. "But it's unlikely he will want to stay on."

She took them down to meet the hotel manager, who invited them to have lunch in the restaurant.

Natasha stopped by the ladies' bathroom, giving Malcolm and Ari a chance to talk alone.

"Looks like you and Miss LeBlanc are finally getting along."

Ari glanced at his father. "I'm just getting to know her."

Natasha joined them at the table. "So what do you think of the hotel, Mr. Alexander?"

"It's nice," he responded. "This hotel served as the model and inspiration of many properties around the world. Robert DePaul exceeded the expectations with this property and is responsible for rejuvenating his family's hotel empire."

"Mr. Alexander, I see you've done your research, as well." She picked up her menu, scanning the restaurant offerings.

Ari couldn't take his eyes off her.

Malcolm cleared his throat noisily, his way of letting Ari know that he'd noticed

what was going on between him and Natasha.

"What are you ordering, Dad?"

"I was thinking of the crab cakes. How
about you, son? You know what you want?"

"No," Ari responded honestly. He hadn't
paid much attention to the menu until now.
"I think I'll just get the crab cakes, as well."

"They're excellent," Natasha said.

Malcolm's cell phone started to ring. He
answered it.

Ari could tell from his side of the conversation that there was something going on
with one of the hotels back home.

Malcolm excused himself to find a private
place to talk.

"How long has your family been into the
hotel business?" Natasha asked.

"My father grew up working in his parents' bed-and-breakfast. After the military,
he decided to open the first Alexander hotel.
I worked there every summer until I was
sixteen years old. That's when I started
working at the Hilton."

"Why did you leave your family's hotel?"
She sampled her vegetables.

"I wanted to get some experience with a
larger chain. I thought it would come in
handy in the future." He reached for his
water glass.

Natasha smiled. "Turns out you were right."

Malcolm left for the airport after lunch. He had planned to stay overnight, but there was an emergency at home with the Alexander Hotel in Douglasville.

Ari and Natasha returned to the penthouse. They settled down in the living room. "When will you and your family transition to Beverly Hills?"

"I'm actually planning to stay out here, but Dad needs to settle things at home before he and Mom move to California permanently. My sister is arranging for my stuff to be packed and shipped to me."

Natasha was confused. "What about your wife?" she blurted. "Your children? When will they arrive?"

Puzzled, he asked, "How did you know I had a wife?"

She pointed to his wedding ring.

"My wife passed away," Ari told her. "We didn't have any children."

"I'm so sorry," she murmured. "I just assumed you were married when I saw your ring."

"I've never taken it off," he responded.

"How long has it been?"

"Two years," he replied.

Her heart skipped a beat upon learning that he was a single man.

She sensed the subtle shift in his mood, so Natasha picked up her pen and said, "I see you're anxious to take the reins, so let's get started."

"Natasha, we really want to make this a smooth transition."

"Well, if there is anything I can do to make your relocation stress free, just let me know."

Ari met her gaze straight on. "Thank you. I'll keep that in mind."

"I think we should schedule a few trips to each of the properties over the next couple of months. It's a good idea for you to get to know the staff. There are going to be some concerns about job security."

"There are going to be some changes in management. I can tell you this much," Ari said. "My brother Blaze will be stepping up as vice president of sales and marketing. My sister Sage will be vice president of residential sales."

"I assume she has a background in real estate."

Ari nodded. "Sage has been involved with real estate since she graduated from college. She will be responsible for the overall sales of the residences and the building of residential teams and infrastructure for the company."

"It sounds like your father has plans to expand the residential offerings." Natasha began making notes on her BlackBerry.

"I trust that what we discuss will be kept in the strictest confidence."

Natasha met his gaze. "Ari, you can trust me."

"I hope so," he commented.

"Tell me about Blaze," she said. "What are his qualifications?"

"He is currently the director of sales and marketing for a chain of grocery stores in Georgia, Florida and South Carolina." He paused a moment before adding, "My father would never hand down promotions we didn't deserve. He is a businessman."

"I had to ask," Natasha replied. "I've seen companies fail because of nepotism. The best way to avoid infringing the rights of workers is to ensure that any employment decisions are based on work-related reasons such as skills, competence and experience rather than blood. Fairness and equality in the workplace will earn the employees' loyalty and dedication."

He agreed. "Now that we are on the same page, there's some information I need right away. I'd like to review all of the licenses and permits for all of the properties. I need to see where everything stands. I'd also like to review the policies-and-procedures manual. I know this isn't your job, but you are all I have right now."

Natasha continued capturing her notes on the BlackBerry. "Have you and your family discussed how you're going to handle the media?" she asked.

"We're going to just pretend they don't exist."

She glanced up at him. "Excuse me?"

Ari chuckled. "I'm only kidding, Miss Le-Blanc. We intend to issue a press release and my father is considering one interview, but that's it. It's not as if the whole world cares about the hotel changing hands."

"That's where you're wrong. People are interested," Natasha said. "Robert DePaul was an iconic figure in the hotel industry. People will want to know more about his son and his grandchildren. Your story is one that most people dream about."

"I guess it is our own rags-to-riches version."

She smiled. "It's actually quite beautiful, I think. I'm really sorry that you never got to meet your grandfather, Ari. He was a wonderful and very generous man. I believe his one true regret was in not contacting Malcolm before his illness. He always talked about how much he had missed out on being a father."

"Sounds like you've known him a long time."

"He gave me my first job while I was in college," she responded. "I adored Robert and his wife."

"What about the rest of his family?" Ari inquired. "What can you tell me about them?"

"Harold and I went to college together. He and Robert weren't very close, but they both loved this business. Harold was devastated when he found out that Robert didn't leave the hotel properties to him."

Ari nodded. "I guess I'd feel the same way if I were in his shoes."

"The rest of the family," Natasha began, "they're pretty nice for the most part, but very reserved."

"They really have the guns out for my dad."

"They are fighting for what they believe should be rightfully their inheritance."

"Do you agree with them?" he asked her.

"It's not for me to agree or disagree, Ari. Robert was in his right mind until the very end. This was his decision, and he made it. End of story."

"Only it's not really the end, Natasha,"

Ari countered. "The DePaul family is out to prove that my father somehow tricked Robert into leaving the properties to him, which we know is not the case. My dad had never met the man, but they will say anything to discredit my father. I am not about to let that happen."

Natasha struggled to maintain a professional front, but she found that she was unable to keep her eyes off the handsome Ari, especially now that she knew he was a single man. She felt sorry that he had lost his wife, and she could tell he still grieved for her.

"What do you love about living in Los Angeles?" Ari asked.

"Driving on Mulholland Drive on a clear day," Natasha responded with a smile. "I love driving out to the beaches."

"Any one in particular?"

She shook her head no. "I just love being near the ocean."

"It's going to take me some time to get used to all the traffic," Ari stated with a frown. "And what's with the couches and televisions on the balconies? You won't see that in Aspen or even Atlanta. When did a balcony become an extension of someone's living room?"

"You will probably see just about anything

out here. L.A.'s cosmopolitan, strange, but also exciting."

Ari's eyes searched Natasha's face, reaching into her thoughts.

"What is it?" she asked. "Why are you looking at me like that?"

"I'm sorry," Ari murmured. "I apologize for staring at you. It's just that you had this expression on your face when you were talking — it reminded me of my late wife. She had that same expression whenever she was in deep contemplation."

"You miss her a lot, don't you?"

He nodded then cleared his throat. "I guess we should get back to work."

Natasha rose to her feet. "I have a couple of projects I need to clear off my desk, so I need to spend a couple of days in my office. I'll check in with you, but I won't be available until Monday. Then I can give you my full attention."

Something flickered in Ari's eyes but disappeared as quickly as it had come, leaving her to wonder what he could be thinking. Natasha couldn't help but wonder if he were always so serious.

CHAPTER 9

Ari couldn't get Natasha out of his mind. She wouldn't be back at the corporate headquarters until Monday. However, this would give him some time alone to conduct research on the permit issue.

Over the next couple of hours, Ari made several phone calls and copies of documents to send to his father. He also met with the human resources department regarding open vacancies they needed to fill immediately.

Natasha called him, checking to see how things were going.

"Do you have any questions for me?" she inquired.

"Not right now."

They talked for about five minutes before Natasha had to answer an incoming phone call.

A fleeting image of April formed in his head and quickly dissipated, leaving behind a thread of guilt. How could he think about another woman when his wife had been dead for only two years?

He and April were born on the same day and had known each other since they were in kindergarten. He remembered the day they met, when he had boldly walked up to her and announced he was going to be her husband one day.

The memory made Ari smile. April was Ari's first and only love. He had no experience with any other woman, so what he was now feeling confused him.

Ari was grateful to have his father with him to provide a buffer between him and Natasha. But what would happen when Malcolm was gone? His father wouldn't be back for a few weeks, leaving him to work closely beside Natasha.

He picked up a book he had been meaning to read for the past couple of weeks. Maybe this would help to take his mind off a certain beautiful woman.

Franklin entered the living room and said, "I would like to say that it will be an honor to serve you and your family."

Ari smiled. "Thank you, Franklin. I have to tell you that we are a hands-on family. My father had planned to talk to you, but he was called away on business. He wanted me to tell you how much he admires loyalty and that, while we have never had a butler, he doesn't want to lose you."

Franklin released the breath he was holding. "I'm sorry. I thought you were terminating my position."

"In a way," Ari said. "Dad wants to place you in charge of all of the housekeeping and security staff. This includes permanent and temporary employees for all of the properties my father now owns. The first thing we would like is for you to have the locks on the house in Pacific Palisades and all security codes changed. My father will discuss the increase in your salary."

"Thank you. I would first like to suggest that the employees travel with your family. I will leave ahead of everyone to determine what will need to be done."

"Sounds good," Ari stated.

Franklin gave him a rare smile. "Thank you, Mr. Ari. I look forward to serving your family."

"Okay, the first thing I want you to do is call me Ari. Just Ari."

He nodded. "If you have need of me, I can be reached by dialing 1-0-1."

"I'll be fine, Franklin. Enjoy your evening."

Ari settled against the deep cushions of

the sofa, the TV remote in hand. Tomorrow, he and Natasha were going to the corporate offices on Wilshire Boulevard and then to the oceanfront home that now belonged to his father. Ari had never been to Pacific Palisades, but he was looking forward to seeing the Pacific Ocean.

Mostly, he was looking forward to spending time with Natasha LeBlanc. Ari still wasn't sure where her loyalties were placed, but he vowed to find out, and the only way to do that was by getting to know her.

The next morning, Natasha met Ari down in the hotel lobby. They were riding over to the corporate offices together, and he wanted to drive out to see the house. She had to be back at her office no later than noon. For the next two days, she had to take care of some urgent deadlines approaching with her other clients.

Natasha was excited about working with Ari. When he wasn't being so serious, she found he had a great sense of humor.

"Is Harold DePaul back in town?" he asked her.

"Yes," she responded, trying not to devour him with her eyes. "He's back. I called his secretary earlier to confirm."

"Great."

"Ari, I can tell you this much — Harold is not going to take this well."

"I hadn't expected that he would," he told her. "However, this transition is going to happen."

Natasha pulled out her BlackBerry.

"What are you doing?" Ari asked. "You're not about to warn him, are you?"

"I'm just checking email," Natasha replied. "What is it going to take for you to believe that I'm on your side, Ari?"

"Time, I suppose," he answered.

She was smiling and radiant. "I'm going to earn your trust, Ari Alexander."

At that moment, all Ari could think about was kissing Natasha. He tore his gaze away from her full lips, which were lightly tinted with lip gloss. He pretended to be engrossed in the document he was reading.

There were moments when his body warmed beneath her gaze. Whenever he caught her staring, Natasha would quickly look away. A secret smile tugged at his lips.

When they arrived to the DePaul Group corporate offices, Natasha told him, "Ari, please give me a few minutes alone with Harold. I've known him a long time and I'd like to speak with him first."

"Why don't we do this together?" he suggested. Ari wasn't sure what she was up to, but he was hesitant to let her face Harold alone.

"I'll be fine," she assured him. "Harold will take the news better if it's just me. He's a very prideful man."

"I'll give you five minutes."

Natasha smiled. "That's all I'll need." She turned and walked briskly down the hallway.

"Natasha, it's good to see you," Harold DePaul said, meeting her outside his office. "So, how did your meeting go? Should I send my secretary to get the champagne?"

"I'm afraid it's not what you want to hear," she responded. Natasha glanced over her shoulder then back at him. "Let's talk in your office."

Harold's face dropped. "What do you mean?"

She waited until they were inside his corner office before saying, "Malcolm decided to keep the hotel properties." Natasha paused a moment before adding, "His son Ari will be assuming your position, effective immediately. He would like you to stay on, but —"

Harold interrupted her by saying, "I'm not about to work for Malcolm Alexander. I don't care what anybody says. That man is a not a DePaul."

"The DNA test says otherwise," Natasha

136

reminded him. "Harold, I know you hate facing the truth, but this man is a part of your family. He is Robert's only son and heir."

Harold muttered a curse. "He's going to ruin everything my uncle has built — his entire empire is going to just crumble down. Uncle Robert clearly wasn't in his right mind."

"You know that's not true."

"Really? Surely, you can't believe my uncle did this with a sane thought in his head. Before his death, his mind became confused with his past and his present. I will testify to this in court, as will my entire family."

Natasha did not respond. She knew what Harold was saying wasn't true, but it was useless to argue with the man.

"We have to get those people out of my family's business. The DePauls have worked too hard to walk away without a fight."

"Malcolm has asked me to stay on as a consultant," she announced. "And Ari is here with me. He's waiting in the reception area."

Harold smiled. "Great. We'll have you working from the inside. I want you to get to know this man and his family. Use your charms if you have to."

She took a step backward. "Excuse me?"

"I want you to tell me everything. I want to know about every decision, everything they make."

"I'm not your spy, Harold," Natasha snapped.

"I guess you forgot about our little deal."

"I haven't forgotten anything, but I'm not going to sneak around the corridors, trying to listen to everything said behind closed doors."

"If you want my money for your son's medical expenses, then you'll do what I say."

They were interrupted by a knock on the door.

Harold opened it to find Ari standing there.

"We were just talking about you," he said, stepping aside to let Ari enter. "I was just telling Natasha that I think it is only fair to let you know that we are not going to contest the will."

Ari shrugged. "If you did, you stand to lose your share of Robert's estate. He made sure the will was irreversible."

"What my uncle did to us is wrong," Harold argued.

"I'm not here to discuss my father's inheritance with you."

"Then what are you here for?" he demanded. "To fire me as managing director?"

"You are welcome to stay on in some capacity, but not in your current position."

Harold stood toe-to-toe with Ari. "Who's going to replace me? *You?*" He laughed harshly. "You don't know a thing about managing a five-star luxury hotel."

Ari didn't flinch at the man's closeness. "You have no idea of my capabilities."

"I will have my office . . . this office cleaned out by tomorrow." Harold folded his arms across his chest. "Just so that you know . . . half of management will be leaving with me. I hope you're prepared for that."

"We are prepared to do whatever is necessary," Ari responded. "If I don't see you here tomorrow when I arrive, I want you to know that I wish you much success in your endeavors. We will be more than happy to provide you with a letter of reference."

"Go to hell," Harold uttered. "I don't need anything from you or your father."

"Well, that went well," Ari stated as they made their way outside the building.

"At least he's not going to contest the will," Natasha said.

"Only because he knows that he and his family wouldn't win, and they would risk losing their inheritance."

The chauffeur immediately got out of the car to open the door for them.

Natasha climbed inside first, followed by Ari. She sat down and began checking her email.

"I wonder what he's up to," he murmured.

"Who?" Natasha asked, looking over at him.

"Harold," Ari answered. "I have a strong suspicion that he's got something up his sleeve. He was acting much too cocky."

"Trust me . . . he's always like that."

"Will you have dinner with me?" Ari blurted before he could stop himself.

"Um, sure." Natasha eyed him.

He grinned. "Did I shock you?"

"I wasn't expecting a dinner invitation from you."

"We're going to have to work together for the next year, so we might as well take this opportunity to get to know one another."

"I agree," she responded. "I need to check in on my staff. When and where do you want to meet?"

"I'm the new guy in town. Do you have any suggestions?"

"Why don't we eat at the Premiere Italiante in Hollywood? Your father owns the restaurant."

"Sounds good," he told her.

"Great. Is seven good enough for you?"

"Sure."

They were headed to Robert's oceanfront estate in Pacific Palisades.

Ari couldn't believe the size of the exquisite Tuscan home in the Palisades Riviera. His grandfather had spared no expense and overlooked no details.

"Robert had this house custom-built a couple of years ago," Natasha said. "There are three levels with nine bedrooms and one down. There are fifteen bathrooms."

"Wow." Ari got out of the limo, followed by Natasha.

"I had Franklin meet us here," she told him. "No one has been in the house in weeks, as far as I know."

"I'm pretty sure Harold has been here," Ari said.

Inside the house, Natasha gave him a tour. "The master suite is located on the first floor. There is an office and library on the first floor.

"As you can see, the gourmet kitchen opens up to the family room. There is a kids' study area on the third floor."

"What did Robert want with such a big house?"

"He never told me, but sometimes it seemed as if he were building the house for your family. Robert talked of inviting all of you out here, so that he could tell your family everything."

Ari and Natasha stepped outside to view the saltwater pool and spa, the outdoor kitchen with barbecue, patio dining area, cozy fireplace and mini sport court. He had to admit, it was the perfect place for their family gatherings.

He counted at least twelve fireplaces total. Ari liked the state-of-the-art gym area, the game room and the home theater that seated fifty. "I can't imagine how much this must have cost Robert."

"Thirty million dollars," Natasha said. "Robert paid for it in cash. He said that he wanted to make sure that the house stayed in the family."

"What are those houses back there?"

"Guesthouses," Natasha explained. "There are four on the property. Each one of them has two bedrooms and two-and-a-half bathrooms."

Ari took pictures with his iPhone. "My parents are not going to believe this house."

Franklin was standing in the kitchen making notes.

"I'll have my parents fax you a shopping list so that you can stock the pantry with their favorites," Ari said. "Everything else is at your discretion. My dad should be calling you with a household budget."

"We spoke fifteen minutes ago. He's authorized a cleaning crew to come in. Mr. Alexander has also requested that I move into one of the villas here. He wants me to manage this property exclusively. Your parents are planning to make this their permanent home."

Ari scanned Franklin's face. "How do you feel about this?"

"I love the ocean."

"Great."

Natasha stood in the doorway of the kitchen. "We should head back, Ari."

He followed her out of the house and to the limo.

"So, I'll see you later," Ari said when they returned to the corporate offices forty-five minutes later.

Natasha slipped her purse on her right shoulder. "Seven o'clock, right?"

He gave a slight nod.

She waved and, with a springy bounce, walked over to her car. Natasha unlocked the door and quickly stepped inside.

Ari watched her drive away, her car quickly disappearing into the heavy traffic.

Natasha hated having to work long hours,

but her job sometimes demanded that she do so. She didn't classify having dinner with Ari as a job, however. She thoroughly enjoyed his company.

At home, she spent some quality time with Joshua and saw if Monica could stay longer.

"I should be back home by nine o'clock, Monica. I'm having dinner with the grandson of Robert DePaul."

"That's fine," the nurse replied. "If you want, I can just spend the night here. This way, you don't have to worry if your meeting runs longer than expected."

Natasha smiled. "You don't mind?"

"Not at all." Monica paused a moment before saying, "Oh, I heard about a new treatment for leukemia. I put the information on the counter for you."

"Thanks," Natasha responded. "I'll take it to Joshua's doctor." Her son had a rare form of leukemia, and the treatment cost thousands of dollars. She didn't care about the expense as long as it kept her son's condition in remission.

She strode into the kitchen to make dinner for Monica and Joshua. The nurse came in to assist her.

"Joshua's teacher loved his story," Monica announced.

Natasha smiled. "He worked hard on it.

I'm glad she liked it. All he ever wants to write about is football. She doesn't seem to mind, though."

"She says as long as he's writing, the subject matter doesn't matter to her. Some of his classmates need writing prompts, but not Joshua."

"He's doing so well in school," Natasha said. "I was worried that Joshua wouldn't be able to keep up."

Monica patted her on the arm. "Joshua is smart, caring and courageous. You should be very proud of how well you've raised him."

"I am proud of him, Monica. I just wish he had a strong male influence in his life. He needs that."

"He will have that, Natasha. One day you're going to meet the right man."

She laughed. "Let's just hope it happens while I'm young enough to appreciate him."

CHAPTER 10

This was a mistake.

Ari paced back and forth across the floor, wondering what he was thinking when he asked Natasha to have dinner with him.

I only invited her because I don't like eating alone.

He knew it was more than that. He was curious about Natasha and since they would be working together, Ari wanted to get to know her better. He wanted to go over some business details, as well.

Ari stood in the middle of the bedroom, trying to decide if he should wear the black suit or the navy blue one. He tried to imagine which one April would've picked.

He smiled. April loved him in black, so she would most likely choose that one. But then again, she always said that navy blue represented honesty.

Ari sighed. "I really miss you, April. I don't know if I can ever love a woman as much as I loved you."

"Not so," his heart whispered back.

He thought of Natasha and considered canceling their dinner meeting. Ari looked at the clock on the nightstand. They were supposed to meet in forty-five minutes. It wouldn't be fair to cancel on her this late.

"Tonight, this is about business," he said to himself. "I can do this."

He removed his shoes and padded barefoot to the bathroom. He would decide on which suit to wear after his shower.

Ari eventually decided to go with the black suit. He stared at his reflection in the mirror. Uncertainty crept into his expression.

He was treading into uncharted territory here. Ari had never felt so drawn to a woman outside of his late wife. How was he going to handle this situation?

I'm definitely not going to allow myself to be sued for sexual harassment.

Ari intended to keep a professional distance where Natasha was concerned. He turned away from the full-length mirror, wearied by indecision. His mind was congested with doubts and fears.

He wished he had followed his decision to cancel out on dinner, but it was too late now.

I can do this, he told himself.

He glanced over at the clock on the night-stand, grabbed his wallet and keys. Ari headed to the door. He took the private elevator down to the lobby.

The concierge approached him, asking, "How can I be of service, Mr. Alexander?"

"I need a taxi, please."

"The limo is available, Mr. Alexander."

He gave a polite smile. "I'd like something a little smaller."

She nodded. "Yes, sir. I'll order a taxi for you."

Five minutes later, Ari was on his way to meet Natasha.

Ari arrived at his destination twenty minutes later.

As soon as Natasha arrived, they were seated.

She looked very fashionable in a silk black-and-pink tunic over a pair of black silk pants. Natasha had a flair with chunky jewelry, Ari observed.

He sat at the table trying to come up with something intelligent to say. *This isn't a date,* he kept telling himself. *It's just a business dinner.*

For some strange reason, it felt more like a date. He had been around scores of beautiful women since April's death, but none had ever made him feel like this.

■ ■ ■ ■

Ari pulled at his shirt collar.

Natasha quietly surveyed the man sitting across from her in the restaurant. This was the fourth time in ten minutes that he'd straightened the collar of his crisp, white shirt. *He's uncomfortable around me,* she decided.

"You look as if you'd rather be anywhere but here with me," she said, sensing his disquiet. "I take it you haven't spent much time with other women since your wife died. It's either that, or I make you uncomfortable."

His eyes registered his surprise.

Natasha pointed at his wedding band and chose her words carefully. "You have the look of a married man written all over you, Ari."

He played with the ring for a moment and then said, "You are the first woman I've had dinner with outside of family since she died. It's . . . it feels a bit strange."

"I can't imagine how you must be feeling after something like that, but you can relax. This dinner is just for us to get to know one another since we're going to be working together. It's not like we're on a date."

Ari nodded. "You must think I'm being foolish."

"Actually, I don't," Natasha responded. "You must have loved her very much."

He smiled. "I *do* love her very much. April is the love of my life and she was my best friend."

Natasha glimpsed a momentary flash of pain in his eyes. She waited patiently to see if he would continue, but Ari remained silent. She chewed her bottom lip as she tried to think of something to say.

"I didn't mean to darken the mood of our dinner," Ari said.

"You haven't," she responded. "Sometimes talking helps the grieving process."

Ari reached for his glass of ice water and took a sip. "They tell you that you'll eventually feel normal again, but for me, it hasn't happened. I still feel like there's a huge part of me missing."

The waitress delivered their food selections to the table.

When she walked away, Natasha announced, "I lost my best friend in a car accident about three years ago. We had been friends since first grade, and when he died, I felt the same way you're feeling. It eventually got better."

"Was he the Wharton alumnus?"

150

"Yes."

"I'm sorry for your loss, Natasha."

She smiled. "Why don't we change the subject?"

Ari chuckled. "Yeah, let's do that." He pointed to his plate. "This is the best crab alfredo I've ever eaten."

"You will have to try the blackened chicken alfredo next time."

His eyes traveled the dining area. "So my dad owns this place?"

"He does. This was one of Robert's favorite places to eat. When the previous owner was thinking of closing the restaurant, your grandfather purchased it. He asked the staff to stay and offered pay increases because he didn't want the menu or the food to change. It paid off for him, because this is one of the most popular Italian restaurants in Los Angeles."

The manager came over to say hello.

"I hope you are enjoying your meal," he told them.

Ari smiled. "I was just telling Natasha that I've never eaten crab alfredo that tasted this good. It was superb."

"Thank you, sir. I am so glad you enjoyed it. The head chef makes the pasta every morning from scratch."

They talked for a few minutes before he

moved on.

"How did he know who I was?" Ari asked in a low voice.

"Maybe it was because you're with me, but I believe it's more your resemblance to Robert." Natasha leaned forward in her seat. "What do you think of the DePaul Beverly Hills property?" She paused a moment. "I'm sorry. It's the Alexander-DePaul Beverly Hills Hotel."

"It's exquisite," Ari exclaimed. "I've been in some really nice hotels, but this particular piece of property is a sight to behold. I love the blend of old-style Hollywood and modern-day luxury."

Natasha took a sip of water. "Your grandfather had an eye for beauty."

"Tell me more about him. All I know of Robert DePaul is what I've read in magazine and newspaper articles."

"He was one of the nicest men I've ever met," Natasha responded with a smile. "I learned a lot about this business from him. Ari, you are a lot like him."

He wiped his mouth, then Ari inquired, "How do you mean?"

"He had worked in hotels since he was strong enough to carry luggage. His parents owned a small one in North Carolina. At the age of sixteen, Robert persuaded his parents to purchase a second hotel in a nearby town. By the time he was eighteen, Robert was managing a third hotel near the beach in Wilmington."

"That's where he met my grandmother," Ari interjected. "She worked as a maid in the Wilmington hotel. According to the letter DePaul wrote to my dad, they fell madly in love, but because of the racial barriers of that time, they kept their relationship a secret. When she found out that she was carrying his child, my grandmother returned to Georgia to avoid any hint of a scandal."

"Robert never stopped loving your grandmother, Ari."

"How do you know that?" Ari inquired, surprised by her words. He knew that she was telling the truth because of what Robert had written to his father.

"He talked about her often during the last months of his life," Natasha replied. "Letting her leave with his child was the hardest decision he had ever made, according to Robert."

"He wrote as much in his letter to my father," Ari said. "I can't help but wonder if he would've felt the same way if he'd had other children."

"I don't know if you'll ever find the answer to that question, Ari. However, I can tell you this. He loved his nieces and nephews like they were his own, but his feelings for them didn't stop him from leaving the bulk of his estate to your father."

"I would have liked to have met him."

"Ari, Robert wanted to get to know all of you. He kept track of your father, but feared it was too late." Natasha wiped her mouth on the end of her napkin. "There's something I think you need to know. Robert went to see your grandmother before she died. She was in the hospital. He flew to be by her side as soon as he heard she was sick."

Ari was completely blown away by this information. His father's reaction would be the same as his, but it was important for Malcolm to know just how much Robert had cared for his mother. "How did he find out?"

"There was only one person who knew your grandmother's secret," Natasha began.

"Had to be Aunt Lena. They were very close. My dad doesn't know about any of this."

Natasha nodded. "I was in a meeting with Robert when she called to tell him about your grandmother. I had never seen him shed a tear until that day."

"Even when his wife died?"

"He was stoic, but there were no tears.

When your grandmother died, Robert returned to Georgia. He waited until everyone left the cemetery to say his final goodbye." Natasha met his gaze. "He loved your grandmother until the very end. I'd like to think that a love like that survives death, and that they are finally together for eternity."

Ari was so quiet that Natasha could only assume he was thinking of his late wife. To end the silence, she asked, "So how did you end up in the hospitality industry? Did you want to follow in your father's footsteps?"

"When the new hotel was being built near my high school, everyone talked about the opportunity for jobs and how cool it would be to work there — even April." Ari smiled. "I badgered them during construction, and they gave me a part-time job. I worked there until I left for college. I would return during breaks from school, and then full-time after graduation."

"So was it as cool as you thought?"

He nodded. "I loved my job. I worked as a waiter. After graduating from college, I became the assistant food and beverage manager. I stayed with that company for another three years. I left because I wanted to work with my parents, but also because I was always number two and I wanted a step up."

"I'm sure they were thrilled," Natasha murmured.

Ari gave a short laugh. "Actually, my father asked me, 'Why should I take you on?' "

She was surprised. "What did you say?"

"I was stumped, so I just responded, 'Why wouldn't you?' He ended up making me a junior assistant reservations manager doing the graveyard shifts. I worked my way up to conferencing and banqueting manager within a year."

"Were you disappointed that he didn't just give you a prestigious position from the beginning? You're the owner's son — that's a perk, isn't it?"

"I don't like the word 'perk,' " Ari responded. "It's sleazy. My father didn't just give me a job. He interviewed me and I had to prove myself just as any other employee. The way I see it, Natasha, being Malcolm Alexander's son is a privilege — not a perk."

"I think it's really sweet you feel that way about your father."

"I was blessed with a wonderful set of parents."

Natasha took a sip of her water. "I feel the same way about my mom and dad. They have always been there for me and my siblings. If they had their way, I would still be in Phoenix."

"Is that where you grew up?"

She nodded. "I miss home, but I love living in Los Angeles."

"This city is very different from what I'm used to," Ari said. "I'm not sure I'll ever get used to so much traffic."

"You will," Natasha assured him. She was secretly thrilled that Ari seemed more at ease around her.

Ari was enjoying his conversation with Natasha immensely.

Natasha picked up her fork. "Tell me about your family, Ari."

"Let's see, you've already met my father. He's a good man and a wonderful role model to my siblings and me. He adores my mother." Ari smiled. "He's the type of man I want to become."

Natasha wiped her mouth with a linen napkin. "I can tell how much you admire him. I think it's great to have someone like that in your life — especially boys. I've always believed boys should have a strong male figure in their lives to teach them how to be a man."

Ari agreed. "Then there's my mother —

she's also a positive role model. She is what some people consider a steel magnolia — a woman who possesses a great sense of humor, intelligence and a quiet strength. People who don't really know her often make the mistake of casting her as a fragile woman, but that soft voice of hers and genteel tone can cut through you like a knife if she feels her family is threatened in any way."

"I can't wait to meet her."

"She's looking forward to meeting you, as well," he told her.

Natasha wiped her mouth with the edge of her napkin. "Okay, so what have you told her about me?"

He grinned. "Just how you snubbed our experience in the hospitality industry."

"You didn't . . ."

Ari laughed. "It's true." His gray eyes widened in accusation. "You said yourself that we didn't have enough experience to manage a chain of luxury spa resorts."

"I shouldn't have been so judgmental."

"It's okay," Ari responded. "We like a challenge."

"I hope your mother doesn't think too badly of me."

"She doesn't," Ari confirmed. "She just wants to meet you. After all, we hired you as our consultant."

"Are any of your other siblings going to work with you and your parents?"

Ari gave a slight shrug. "Drayton is a CPA and he's going to go into business for himself. Kellen and Zaire are still in graduate school, but she's about to graduate. She wants to get into the management training program."

"Wonderful," she responded. "It's one of the best in the industry. I actually considered majoring in accounting when I was in college."

"I can see that in you."

She laughed. "Oh, really?"

He broke into a grin. "Yes, you look like a numbers person."

"Do I?"

Ari nodded.

"So, what is Kellen studying?"

"He's completing his master's in architectural engineering."

Natasha sipped her iced tea. "I can't wait to meet all of them."

"What about you? Do you have any brothers or sisters?"

"I have a brother and sister," Natasha responded with a smile. "We're triplets, actually."

"Are you identical? You and your sister?"

She shook her head no. "Fraternal."

"Are you close?"

Natasha broke into a smile. "We are. My sister was here in Los Angeles until six months ago. She's getting married to her high-school sweetheart, so she's back in Phoenix. My brother also lives in Phoenix."

"Have you ever been married?"

She shrugged nonchalantly. "Yes, but it didn't work out. We were going in two different directions."

"Did it have anything to do with you being a career woman?" Ari inquired. "It doesn't bother me, but I know some men can't handle that."

"It was more that he didn't want to be a husband or a father."

"You have a child?"

Natasha smiled. "A little boy."

"How old is he?"

"He's six years old," she answered. "Joshua is my pride and joy."

"I can tell," Ari said. "Just the mention of his name puts a huge smile on your face. I think it's wonderful. I have always wanted children."

"Being a parent is great. I love him more than my own life."

They talked all through dinner about parenting, sports and business.

Natasha wiped her mouth on the edge of her napkin. "This was a good idea."

"What? Having dinner together?"

She nodded. "I've learned quite a bit about you this evening."

Ari grinned. "Same here."

Natasha leaned forward and asked, "So, am I as bad as you thought?"

"Not at all," Ari confessed over the rapid beating of his heart. "I think you and I are going to be good friends."

"Until I get you on a basketball court," she teased.

"Okay, that just sounded like a challenge," Ari responded. "Natasha, you don't want to do that. I'm just saying."

There was a flurry of activity going on at the corporate office when Ari arrived the next morning.

"What's going on?" he asked.

"Harold's having his stuff moved," came the reply of one of the executive assistants.

Ari surveyed the boxes in the lobby. "He had this much to move?"

The young woman shifted from one foot to the other. "I guess so." She lowered her voice to a whisper and added, "Security arrived about forty-five minutes ago."

Ari read her name tag. "Thank you, Tammie."

She gave him a smile and then took off briskly down the hall.

He had notified building security that Harold might try to take company files with him, and he wanted him detained.

Harold confronted Ari. "How dare you summon security on me. I really hope that you don't consider this some sort of victory, because it isn't. I'm just not willing to stay on and watch this hotel lose its five-star rating."

Ari's voice hardened. "Your uncle apparently lacked faith in your ability, Harold. Otherwise, I'm sure he wouldn't have had any problems leaving the properties in your hands, wouldn't you agree?"

"He wasn't in his right mind," Harold uttered in a nasty tone. "The man was a raving lunatic right before he died."

"That's not what we were told by his attorney," Ari responded. "Robert DePaul was of sane mind when he changed his will."

"That snake will say anything for a handsome check. Oh, and nice touch — locking me out of my uncle's house."

"The house belongs to my father. There is no reason for you to be there."

"If you and your family think you can do

a better job than I did —"

"Harold, a successful hotel requires people, product and performance," Ari interjected. "My father will ensure that the hotels continue to meet and exceed guest expectations."

Harold stalked out of the lobby, fuming.

His cell phone rang.

It was Natasha.

"How are things?" she inquired.

Ari gave her a quick rundown of his conversation with Harold.

"I'm so sorry you had to deal with all that," Natasha said to Ari.

He shrugged in nonchalance. "It doesn't bother me. The man is bitter, and I guess I can understand why. He devoted his life to his uncle's company, and now he's left with nothing."

"He has the two million dollars Robert left him," Natasha said. "This doesn't include the money he inherited from his grandfather.

"So, other than that, is everything going well?"

"They are," Ari answered. "As far as I can tell."

He was pretty sure that there were still a few spies for Harold on the payroll, but he was determined to flush them out.

"Well, I just wanted to check in with you," Natasha said. "I'll see you on Monday."

"Great," Ari responded, walking into the office Harold had vacated.

After he hung up with Natasha, Ari set up a meeting with the head of security at the building. He wanted certain precautions in place.

There was a knock on the door just as he ended the call. It was Tammie, one of the three executive assistants still remaining. She slipped into the office and stood until he gestured for her to sit down.

"Mr. Alexander, I just wanted to inform you that I was the one who called Franklin this morning."

"You wanted him to let me know that Harold was packing up the office."

She met his gaze. "I felt you should know."

"You were right," he told her. "Thank you."

Ari studied her face and then asked, "How are you related to Franklin?" She had the same deep-chocolate coloring and thick, naturally arched eyebrows as Franklin.

She gasped in surprise.

"You have his eyes and his nose," Ari explained. "I have a good memory for faces."

"He's my father."

"Did Robert know?"

"Yes. He hired a detective to look for me and my mom after Franklin came to work for him. Before then, the last time I saw my father was when I was ten years old. He left home one day and never came back." She spoke with light bitterness.

"Tammie, I'm glad to have you on board."

"Mr. DePaul . . . Harold offered me a lot of money to keep an eye on you and your family. I turned him down because it wasn't right, and because I am not motivated by money."

"I appreciate your honesty."

"Mr. . . . Harold did things that weren't quite on the up-and-up around here. He and I didn't really get along. He actually fired me when Mr. Robert got sick but was forced to keep me on by his brother, William. I've worked with William for the past year. He's over in the supply management division. He has been in the hospital. He had a heart attack the week after Mr. Robert died. He's at home recuperating."

"How is he doing?" Ari inquired.

"Much better," Tammie responded as she turned and walked toward the door. "You will need to hire an assistant. Kelly left with Harold."

Ari smiled at her. "Thank you, Tammie."

She paused a moment before opening the door. "William DePaul is nothing like his brother. The two of them didn't get along, but I don't know what William will decide. He respected his uncle greatly."

"Tammie, are you looking to stay where you are?"

"I am very happy to have a job. William and I work well together, but if he decides to leave then I would like to work in accounting." She gave a tiny smile. "I'm going to school at night to become an accountant."

"Really? I have a brother who will be opening up a firm in Los Angeles. We would hate to lose you, but I believe you would be an asset to him."

"That would be wonderful," she gushed, then said, "I'd better get back to work."

Chuckling, Ari turned on the computer monitor.

"The man had the nerve to send security to watch me as I packed up my property — *my property*," Harold fussed. "I wasn't even allowed to take my laptop."

"It belongs to the company, remember?"

Harold gazed at her hard. "I am a DePaul."

Natasha was secretly impressed by the way

Ari had handled Harold.

"How is William?" Natasha asked, changing the subject.

"He's fine."

He began pacing the floor of her office. "I am not going to just let Malcolm Alexander and his spawn have my hotels without a fight," he mumbled.

"They are not your hotels," Natasha pointed out.

He sent her an angry glare.

"As much as you don't want to hear it, Harold, your uncle made his choice of successor."

"It is not that simple," Harold argued. "Look, we have another chance. All you have to do is convince Malcolm to take the company public."

"I'm not sure he will consider —"

He cut her off by saying, "You are his consultant. Natasha, all you have to do is get him to see that it's the right decision and best for the company."

She knew he wanted the hotel group to go public so that he could buy up shares and force a hostile takeover. Natasha wasn't sure she wanted to have any part of this.

"I hope you will keep up your part of our agreement."

"I have kept my part of it," she argued.

"Harold, I can't make Malcolm do anything — all I can do is offer suggestions. It's his decision. He has the final say."

"If you want this money for those precious treatments for Joshua, you had better find a way to convince him."

Harold made his way to the door. "I'll be in touch, Natasha. You remember what I've said."

His words left her shaken. What had she gotten herself into?

Chapter 11

"What was the redevelopment cost of the San Francisco property?" Ari asked. He was glad to have Natasha back. He had missed her.

"I believe it was around twelve million dollars," Natasha responded. "The facilities program includes one hundred unique rooms, an upscale eight-thousand-square-foot spa, six thousand square feet of retail space and an exclusive restaurant."

"The restaurant is an important component of that development," Ari interjected.

Natasha agreed. "It's expected to gross two million." She paused a moment, then said, "I owe you an apology."

"For what?"

"I was wrong when I said you weren't capable of managing this company. You are doing surprisingly well. I never should have doubted your abilities."

He broke into a grin. "Apology accepted,

but it's only been a few days."

"I thought you'd be overwhelmed, but you're not." Natasha checked her watch. "Oh, it's time for the conference call with your parents."

As soon as they had his mother and father on the line, Ari gave them updates on everything that had been done so far. "His brother, William, is still on the payroll. He had a heart attack and is still recuperating."

"I'll reach out to him sometime next week," Malcolm stated.

"I'm actually going to see him later this afternoon," Natasha offered. "I'll schedule a day and time for you."

"That would be great," Malcolm responded.

They were on the phone for about forty-five minutes. When the call ended, Ari rose to his feet and stretched.

"So your brother and sister are flying in to help you," Natasha said. "I think that's great."

"I do, too. There's a lot of work to do."

Natasha had grown quiet.

"Hey, are you okay?" Ari inquired.

"I'm fine."

He wasn't sure he believed her. She was fine until the conference call. He wondered what had happened to change her mood.

Natasha left fifteen minutes later to meet with her employees regarding one of her other clients. Ari used this time alone to make some phone calls and review the information on the Nevada hotels.

"I'm looking at a copy of the permit right now," he said to the clerk at Las Vegas Building Services. After a moment, he added, "I'll fax them over to you."

He hung up and scratched his ear. *Something isn't right about all of this.*

Ari called his father. "Dad, they're saying that we never had permits for the remodeling, but I'm looking at them right now."

"Son, that's strange. They must have misplaced them."

"I don't know what happened, but I'm going to fax what we have over to them right now. I just wanted to give you an update."

They talked a few minutes more before ending the call.

Ari faxed over documents to the City of Las Vegas Building Services.

Natasha called a few minutes later.

"Have you had lunch yet?" she asked.

He smiled at the sound of her voice. "No, I haven't."

"Why don't you meet me at the Takami Sushi & Robata Restaurant on Wilshire? It's not too far from the office. You can just take a taxi there, or you can use the limo. You do like sushi, don't you?"

"I love sushi, but I'll pass on the limo," he said with a chuckle. "Not my style. I need to look into renting a car until mine arrives."

"Why don't you have Tammie arrange it for you?" Natasha inquired.

"I guess I could do that."

"That's what she's there for, Ari. Tammie is very good at her job, and she is there to assist you."

"Got it," he responded. "What time should I meet you?"

"In about thirty minutes," Natasha said. "Will this work for you?"

"Sure. I'll see you then.

"Tammie, could you arrange a rental car for me? Nothing fancy," Ari stated before he left for the restaurant. "I just need something to drive until my own car arrives."

"I'll get right on it."

"Thank you, Tammie."

Ari took a taxi to the address Natasha had given him.

She was waiting inside the lobby.

He glanced around. "Where is the restaurant?"

She smiled. "It's on the twenty-first floor."

They rode the elevator up to the penthouse that housed the restaurant.

"This view is spectacular," Ari commented.

"I love coming here," Natasha confessed. "Great ambiance, and the food is excellent."

He looked over the menu. "What do you recommend?"

"How about the Takami edamame for starters? My favorite entrée is the chicken teriyaki. Ari, you have to try the baked king crab roll and the spicy tuna." She grinned. "They're awesome. If you have room for dessert, then you should try the chocolate lava cake. Yummm."

Amused, Ari enjoyed seeing this side of her. He laid down his menu when their waiter approached the table. "I'm going to let the lady order for me."

It didn't take long for the appetizers to arrive.

Ari sampled the sautéed soybeans in garlic butter and soy sauce. "This is delicious. What is this called again?"

"It's the Takami edamame," Natasha replied. "Wait until you try the baked king crab roll. Ari, you're going to love it."

He enjoyed everything Natasha ordered.

"So which did you like best?" she asked.

"I'd have to say it was the baked king crab roll."

His phone started to vibrate. Ari checked it and said, "That was Tammie. My rental car has been delivered."

"So what type of car did you rent?"

"I don't know for sure. I just told her that I didn't need anything fancy. Just something with four wheels that will get me around the city until my car arrives."

"You're having it transported here?"

"Yes," Ari replied. "It should be here by the end of the week. I wasn't sure if I was going to sell it or give it to my brother. I decided to keep it."

"You look like an SUV type of man."

He smiled. "I am."

"Let's see . . . do you drive an Escalade?"

Ari shook his head. "I'm not much for fancy cars. I drive a Land Rover."

"Nice car, or should I say truck. I looked into getting one, but it drove like a truck. I didn't like that."

"That may be why I like it so much," he responded with a smile.

Their main courses arrived.

"How are you enjoying your job so far?" Natasha inquired as they enjoyed their meal.

"I'm enjoying it," Ari responded. "It is a little different being over at the corporate offices and not at the hotel in the center of everything, but I'm getting used to it."

"You will be spending a lot of time on the road, visiting all of the properties. You may soon appreciate being in a real office."

When they returned to the corporate offices, Ari got out of Natasha's car, pointed to a Bentley Continental GTC convertible and said, "Now that's a car."

"It's a very nice car," Natasha murmured. "You're going to love driving it."

"Excuse me?"

"It's your rental car."

He stood there a moment, tongue-tied. Ari shook his head. "I don't think so."

"It's yours," she countered. Natasha was trying to keep from laughing but failing miserably. "You should see the look on your face. Ari, this isn't a bad thing. The car is gorgeous. Robert enjoyed the finer things in life, and so do all of the hotel guests. Soon, you will, too."

"Do you know how much a car like that costs?"

"I do," she murmured.

He shook his head in denial. "That can't be a rental car . . . my rental car."

The concierge met them at the door. "Mr. Alexander, your rental car is parked outside and ready."

Ari stared at the keys to the Bentley. After a moment, he accepted them from the young woman. "Beth, thank you."

"If you are not leaving anytime soon, I can have a valet park it for you."

Ari handed her the keys. "I won't be leaving until after six."

Beth gave a slight nod. "I'll have someone park the car near the entrance at 6:00 p.m."

"The company has an exclusive contract with Beverly Hills Rent-A-Car," Natasha explained. "They specialize in Bentleys, BMWs, Mercedes and Jaguars . . . those types of cars."

"I don't even want to know how much this is costing the company."

She patted his arm. "No, I don't think you do."

"I was thinking Enterprise, Hertz . . ."

Natasha shook her head. "*Exclusive* contract."

"You wouldn't happen to know when it's up for renewal?"

She gave in to her laughter.

They sat down in his office facing each other. As their eyes met, Ari felt a shock run through him. Clearing his throat, Ari turned on his computer. "I didn't know you could rent a Bentley."

"Wait until you drive it," she assured him. "You're going to fall in love."

"I don't want to fall in love with it. I

would never buy a car like that."

"You'll be surprised what you will do when you have the money to do it."

"My dad has money," he corrected. "I'm doing okay, but I don't roll like that."

She gave him a sidelong glance.

"Okay . . . I'm doing better than okay, but it doesn't mean that I intend to go out and purchase a luxury car like that. I'm a save-for-a-rainy-day type of man."

"I like that," she said. "I'm the same way, although I do have a weakness for a Mercedes-Benz. I've always wanted to own one."

"I have to admit that yours is nice," he told her. "It's *very* nice."

"Thank you."

"What are you reading?" Ari asked when he glimpsed a book in her tote.

"It's the new book by James Patterson."

"*Swimsuit?*"

Natasha was surprised. "You read him?"

Ari nodded. "He's a favorite of mine. I'm a huge mystery reader."

"So am I." She grinned. "He's definitely my favorite author. I've read everything he's ever written."

"We have that in common," he responded.

A soft gasp escaped her. "I never thought I'd hear those words come out of your mouth."

Ari chuckled. "Me, either."

Natasha had brought his long-dead senses back to life. Everything took on a clean brightness when she was around. He found that he truly enjoyed her company.

"Are you listening to me?"

He turned his attention to Natasha. "I'm sorry. What were you saying?" Ari found that she consumed most of his thoughts these days. He was still stunned by his intense attraction to Natasha — a woman he wasn't sure he could trust.

Now that all of the employees loyal to the DePaul family had cleared out, Ari decided it was time to call a staff meeting with the remainder of the executive team.

Natasha had conferenced Malcolm in to discuss the future of the Alexander-DePaul Hotel Group.

After the meeting, Ari spent some time with the PR department to go over the press release that would be going out within the hour.

He waited until everyone left his office.

Ari pushed away from the desk and walked over to the window. He stood there admiring the picturesque view of the city.

He had accomplished a lot in two weeks.

Ari had had the hotel website updated with job openings. Ari also had the job openings posted in the *L.A. Times.* He was moving forward.

"I never imagined we'd be able to get so much done in two weeks," Natasha said when she entered the corner office.

"We still have so much left to do," he said. "But I have a sinking feeling that Harold took some files we may need in the future."

"Security was watching his every move," Natasha told him. "At least that's what you told me."

"He still had plenty of time to destroy information."

"Harold loves the hotels too much to sabotage them," Natasha countered. "I just don't believe he would ever do anything like that."

"I don't trust the man," Ari said.

"You don't have to worry about Harold," Natasha assured him. "He would never do anything to hurt this company."

Ari gave her a look that clearly showed he didn't believe her.

CHAPTER 12

Natasha sat down on the sofa and pulled out her BlackBerry. "I think that once your family is in place, we should host a huge gala for members of the press, celebrities and other dignitaries as a formal introduction of the Alexander-DePaul Hotel Group. But not only that — we need to formally introduce your family. You are now the Alexanders of Beverly Hills."

"You're kidding, right?" Ari asked.

She folded her arms across her chest. "No, actually I'm very serious."

"We don't do galas, Natasha," he responded. "We are more of a down-home-barbecue kind of family."

"Well, you're in Beverly Hills now."

Ari shrugged in nonchalance. "Doesn't matter. We are not about to let money change who we are and what we stand for."

"This chain of hotels has a reputation for being the finest in luxury. They have all earned some of the world's most prestigious awards and are unquestionably the pinnacle of resorts. The Beverly Hills property alone has —"

"Despite earning the Five Diamond Award five years in a row, being voted one of the top 500 Best Hotels and appearing on the Gold List of the World's Best Places to Stay, the hotels are not an extension of our family," Ari interjected. "I agree with you on the hotel's reputation, and my family won't do anything to tarnish that reputation, but we do not intend to change who we are, Natasha. We do enjoy a good party — however, we're not about tuxedos and ball gowns."

"I think you'd look handsome in a tuxedo." The words flew out of her mouth before she could stop them.

Ari broke into a grin. "You really think so?"

"Can we just forget I said that?" Natasha asked. "I didn't really mean to say it out loud."

"You can't take it back," he teased.

Their eyes met and held for a moment.

It was Ari who finally broke the connection. He got up and began to pace back and forth.

Natasha detected a shift in his mood. She

surveyed him for a moment before saying, "We've done enough for today."

He turned around to face her. "Huh?"

She smiled. "We're playing hooky for the rest of the afternoon."

"Where are we going?" Ari asked.

"I think you need some recreation, so we're going to do something fun." Natasha rose to her feet and began packing up her laptop computer. "C'mon."

He smiled. "You're really serious?"

Natasha nodded. "Have you done anything besides work since moving to Los Angeles?"

Ari shook his head no.

"That's what I thought." She gestured toward the door. "Let's get out of here."

Natasha could hardly believe she was asking a client to play hooky with her. *I am losing all perspective where Ari is concerned.*

For a brief second, she considered backing out, but Ari really looked as if he needed to get out of the office.

She didn't tell him that they were going to the beach. Natasha wanted to surprise him.

"Where are you taking me?" Ari questioned. "We're heading to Santa Monica."

"We're going to the pier."

"The Santa Monica Pier," he murmured. "I heard that it was really pretty at night."

182

"It is," she confirmed. "But you looked like you really needed some downtime. Besides, wasn't it you who said that you can't work all of the time? People need to have fun every now and then."

She pulled into a parking lot.

"The water is so beautiful here," Ari murmured. "I had planned to come to the beach at some point, but I'm glad we're here now. It's a perfect day for it."

"I'm glad to hear that," Natasha responded. "I love coming out here when I'm in search of inspiration."

"I can see why."

Ari and Natasha removed their shoes and walked along the sandy strip of land, talking.

"I can't wait for Blaze and Sage to arrive. Maybe then, I'll be able to see my desk."

"I'm looking forward to meeting your brother and sister," Natasha said.

She stepped on something hard and then started to fall.

Almost instinctively, Ari captured her in his arms. "You okay?"

"I'm just embarrassed more than anything." The warmth of his embrace ignited a wave of desire through Natasha.

"This is nice."

"What is?" Natasha asked, trying to keep

her voice neutral.

"Being out here with you." He paused a moment, then said, "I'm enjoying myself."

"I'm glad," she murmured.

Ari seemed more at ease, which pleased her. It was good to see him more relaxed and not so focused on work.

"I can't believe we've been here for two hours," Ari said. "It didn't seem that long to me."

"You really needed some downtime."

"You're right, Natasha." He glanced around. "I needed this."

"I love coming out here," Natasha told him. "Especially around sunset. The view is absolutely gorgeous."

"I bet," Ari responded.

"So how are you adjusting to your new lifestyle?"

Ari chuckled. "It's pretty strange to have someone waiting on me. Franklin . . . he weirds me out. Don't get me wrong. The dude is cool, but he just appears out of nowhere. I'm glad he will be at the house in Pacific Palisades."

Natasha burst into laughter.

"He seems like a really nice guy, though."

"He is," she responded. "Franklin is loyal. He will be an asset to your family. I don't know if you know this already, but Tammie is his daughter."

"I figured it out," he responded. "She looks just like him."

Natasha checked her watch. "I guess we should head back. We don't want to get caught in rush-hour traffic."

"Thanks for this break," Ari said as they headed back in the direction of the parking lot. "I really needed to get out of that office for a while. I'd like to show my appreciation by cooking dinner for you."

She was surprised by his words. "Really? You can cook?"

Ari nodded. "I actually enjoy it. I've been told that I'm a good cook."

"You are a man of many talents, I see," responded Natasha.

"I'm thinking you should come by around seven."

"Sounds good."

Natasha dropped him off at the hotel thirty minutes later.

"See you in a couple of hours," she told him before driving away.

"Looking forward to it."

I can't believe Ari is cooking me dinner. Natasha stifled her happiness. This was probably just another business meeting. Despite the long looks he gave her, Ari never once hinted at his attraction to her.

Maybe it was all in her head. Maybe Ari wasn't interested in her in that way. Natasha released a long sigh.

In the residence, Ari conducted a quick search of the kitchen to see if he had everything he needed.

Ricardo said, "If you'd like, just give me a menu and I'll prepare everything for your dinner."

"Thanks, but tonight I'll be cooking."

The chef looked disappointed, so Ari explained, "I would like to try and impress Miss LeBlanc with my cooking skills."

Ricardo smiled. "I understand."

Ari wasn't sure why he'd been so transparent with Ricardo, but it was the truth. He wanted to impress Natasha.

He had Ricardo sample the food when it was ready.

"I am impressed," the chef told him. "Where did you learn to cook like this? You went to culinary school, yes?"

"I've taken some cooking classes, but nothing on the line of what you can do. Ricardo, you belong in a restaurant — your own restaurant."

"This is a dream of mine," Ricardo confessed.

Ari made a mental note to talk to his

father. "I guess I'd better shower and change. Natasha will be arriving soon."

He had just finished getting dressed when she arrived, looking stunning in a black maxi dress with spaghetti straps.

Ricardo had transformed from chef to waiter for the evening. "This is my gift to you," he whispered to Ari as he ushered them into the dining room.

"How did you become such an excellent cook?" Natasha asked after trying the scampi.

"I took over the cooking when my wife first got sick. I didn't want her to worry about taking care of me — I just wanted her to get well. It was very relaxing, so after she died, I took cooking classes." Ari took a sip of wine and then swallowed. "Sometimes, I would go into the kitchen at our hotel and help prepare meals."

"You must really enjoy it."

"I do," he said. "It's how I relieve my stress."

"What will you do now since you have an award-winning chef at your disposal?"

"I won't be needing him." Ari smiled at her. "But my parents may feel differently, although my mother is an outstanding cook. I'm sure my dad will be more than happy to give him a great reference, but he won't need it. He's a great chef."

"Why not make him the head chef at the restaurant in Marina Del Rey? Stacy is the chef there now, and she's getting married in a few weeks and moving to France after the wedding."

"This is perfect timing," Ari stated. "I was going to talk to my father about Ricardo taking over one of the restaurants."

She held up a glass of wine and said, "Great minds think alike. At least that's what I've always heard."

Ari tapped his glass to hers. "Looks like we make a great team."

CHAPTER 13

Ari was finding it hard to keep his emotions at bay. It had been a long time since he'd felt so close to a beautiful woman — the only other one being his beloved April. Since her death, he focused on his work as a way to ease his grieving. Ari had never considered that the time would come when another woman would ignite a spark of desire within him. He wasn't prepared for the way Natasha made him feel.

Just being here in this room with her sent a course of electricity within him. Ari tried to shake off the feeling of being so alive, but he failed. The part that he thought had died with April rose up in him and refused to be ignored.

After they finished their meal, Ari and Natasha settled down in the living room.

"Thank you for such a delicious dinner," she told him.

Ari met her gaze and couldn't look away,

feeling that there was a deeper significance to the visual interchange. He pulled her toward him and kissed her, surprising them both. Heat sparked in the pit of his stomach and ignited into an overwhelming desire.

He kissed her a second time; his tongue traced the soft fullness of Natasha's lips.

She gave herself freely to the passion of his kiss, matching him kiss for kiss. It had been a long time since she felt a man's lips on her own.

Ari's mouth covered hers hungrily until reluctantly he released her.

The kiss left Natasha weak and confused.

"Natasha, I'm sorry. I hope I haven't offended you," Ari said quietly. "I have no idea what came over me."

Natasha cleared her throat and gave a nervous chuckle. "It was probably the wine. I recall you saying that you have never been much of a drinker."

"I suppose we could pretend that the kiss never happened, then," he suggested.

She nodded stiffly.

His senses reeled as if short-circuited, but he tried to display an outward calm, despite the physical reactions to his desire for Natasha.

"Maybe we should call it a night," Ari suggested.

She agreed. "Too much wine . . ."

He escorted Natasha to the door. "I really didn't mean to ravish you like that."

She placed a hand to his mouth and said, "We're both adults. We're fine, Ari."

Natasha opened her purse and pulled out her keys. "Good night."

When she was gone, he strode back into the kitchen. Ari picked up the bottle of wine, which was still three-quarters full.

Natasha relived the kiss she shared with Ari over and over in her mind for the rest of the evening and most of the night.

The next morning had come much too quickly for her, but it was time to get out of bed. Natasha crawled from beneath the covers and made her way to the bathroom for a quick shower.

After she got dressed, Natasha walked down the hall to her son's room. He was still sleeping.

She kissed him on the forehead.

He stirred and his eyes opened. "Mommy . . ."

"I'm leaving for work, but I will see you this afternoon when you go in for your treatment."

He started to cry. "I don't wanna go . . ."

"I know, baby, but it will make you all better. It's already working."

"I always get sick, Mommy. I don't like it." Joshua's eyes filled with tears. "I don't wanna go."

"The treatment will help to kill the cancer, baby. Hey, you know I'll be right there with you."

He wrapped his tiny arms around her. "I love you, Mommy."

"I love you more."

Wiping his face with the back of his hand, Joshua gave her a tiny smile. "I love you the mostest."

Monica arrived just as she made her way down the stairs.

"Joshua has chemo today, so I'll meet you at the hospital at three," Natasha told her as she grabbed her keys. "He's a little anxious about it. Joshua doesn't like the way it makes him feel."

Monica nodded. "I understand. I'll talk to him and see if he has any questions or just wants to vent."

"You're so good with him."

"He's such a sweetheart," Monica complimented. "I love him like he was one of my own children."

Natasha left the house and drove to her office. She met with her staff for about an hour, made a few phone calls and then headed to the Alexander-DePaul corporate headquarters.

She decided she would follow Ari's lead. If he acted as if nothing had happened between them, then so would she.

Her cell phone rang.

She saw that it was Harold who was calling and let it go to voice mail. She was in no mood to deal with one of his temper tantrums. Natasha was well aware of what she had to do.

When she arrived, Ari was in business mode, so she pushed all thoughts of the kiss to the back of her mind.

They were in his office talking about the future of the company. "I would love to expand to the East Coast," Ari mentioned.

"Maybe you should talk to your father about taking the company public," Natasha suggested. This was the perfect time to bring up the subject. "It will result in increased capital and create a type of currency in the form of its stock that the company can use to make other acquisitions. It's something I think your family should seriously consider." Natasha paused a moment before adding, "Robert was thinking of selling off shares of the company before he got sick."

Ari didn't respond.

"You've gone quiet on me," she said.

"What are you thinking?"

"What you're saying sounds pretty good, Natasha, but I'm not sure it's the right move for us. Going public is an expensive process and if the offering does not go through, the company will lose that money. Another disadvantage is that the decision-making process becomes more formal and less flexible when there are shareholders. More importantly, this would also put the company at risk of takeover attempts."

"I would certainly advise you to implement certain antitakeover measures," Natasha stated. "It's just another option."

"So noted," Ari said. A smile tugged at his lips.

"I've heard that you have made a tremendous impression on the staff here."

Ari shrugged. "I am just being myself. The employees are wonderful, and as long as they do the work they were hired to do, I'm happy."

"Apparently, they are thrilled to have someone fair and objective in leadership."

"My grandfather hired some of the best, from what I can tell."

Natasha nodded. "He did. Robert always said that the hotel clientele demanded quality in every area, and he intended to give them their money's worth."

"This is as it should be," Ari stated.

Feeling like a traitor, Natasha made up an excuse to leave Ari's office.

I can't believe I just sat there and lied to Ari that Robert was considering taking his company public.

The truth of the matter was that Harold had approached his uncle with the idea, but Robert quickly nixed the suggestion for pretty much the same reasons Ari had stated.

As soon as she arrived back to her office, Natasha checked in with her assistant before heading into her office and closing the door.

She placed a call to Harold.

"I did what you asked," Natasha told him when he answered the phone.

"How did it go?"

"Surely you didn't expect a decision this soon," she responded. "Harold, I didn't like lying about your uncle. None of this feels good to me."

"Just think of your little boy and what those treatments will mean to him."

Natasha kept her temper in check.

"In a few days, you should follow up with Malcolm. Forget that idiot son. He will be the one to make the decision, after all."

"That's all I wanted to say," she stated. "I have a meeting in a few minutes, so I need to prepare."

"Natasha . . ."

"Goodbye, Harold." Natasha disconnected the call.

She settled back in her chair and closed her eyes. *I never should've gotten involved in this thing between Malcolm and Harold, but it's too late now.*

She was falling hard for Ari, and she felt terrible for what she was doing to his family.

Natasha placed her fingers to her mouth. Ari's kiss had marked her for life. No man had ever kissed her so passionately.

I don't deserve a man like Ari. How could I betray his trust like this?

She already knew the answer.

I would do anything to save my baby's life, including help Harold.

The next day, Sage and Blaze arrived on the private plane. Ari didn't meet them at the airport but had arranged for them to be picked up by the DePaul chauffeur. He was glad they were there.

The chauffeur had called him ten minutes ago to let Ari know that they were only minutes away from the hotel. He took the private elevator downstairs.

The limo had just pulled up in front of

196

the hotel entrance.

Ari greeted his siblings.

"I don't know if I can ever fly domestic again," Sage told him. "Flying on a private plane is definitely the way to go."

Blaze nodded in agreement. "The flight was smooth."

He walked beside them while the chauffeur took care of Blaze's and Sage's luggage.

"This hotel is gorgeous," Sage exclaimed, her eyes bouncing around the lobby area. "I can't believe this is all ours."

Ari and Blaze chuckled.

She turned around to look at her brothers. "You can laugh all you want. I'm still pinching myself. We're rich."

"No, Sage," Ari corrected. "Dad and Mom are wealthy."

"Hey, it's part of our inheritance," Sage countered. "In case you've forgotten, this is going to be a family business."

"We work for Dad," Blaze interjected. "All of this belongs to them."

"You have always been a party pooper," she said.

He chuckled as he led the way to the private elevator.

When Sage walked into the penthouse, she looked around in awe. "I could really get used to living like this," she murmured. "Dad said I could pick out one of the residences as my own."

"I'm going to check out some of the condos on Wilshire Boulevard," Blaze stated. "I'm not like you and Ari. I don't want to live where I work."

Sage laughed. "You just don't want Mom and Dad in your business."

"You're right," he responded. "Mostly, I don't want all of you nosing around. I had enough of that when we were growing up."

Sage waved her hand in dismissal. "We're just trying to look out for you. I know I don't want some woman trying to use you or mistreat you." She strolled around the room, looking at and touching the furnishings. "I'm very protective of my family."

Ari smiled. His sister was telling the truth. Sage had always been protective of them.

Blaze walked over to the window and peered out. "Now, this is what I call a room with a view."

Sage and Blaze settled down in the living room with Ari.

"So, bring us up to speed," Blaze said. "What's going on around here? Dad told us that the nephew and employees loyal to him all left the company."

Ari nodded in agreement. "He's got them

convinced that there won't be a hotel left after we're done. He told them that we didn't know what we were doing."

"He said that?" Sage asked.

"Yeah," Ari responded. "He practically said it to my face."

"I think it's pretty obvious that he's a fool," Sage interjected. "He has no idea what a smart businessman our father is, and he clearly knows nothing about you."

Ari shrugged in nonchalance. "It doesn't matter. I think it's best that he's not working with us. We could never trust the man."

"Blaze and Sage are here with me," Ari announced when he reached Natasha on the phone an hour later. "I was wondering if you could join us for dinner."

"I wish I could, but I won't be able to make dinner tonight," Natasha responded. "I have other plans, but how about lunch on Monday?"

"Sure," he replied. She had been acting strangely since they shared that kiss. Now she seemed to be avoiding him.

Ari worried that he'd misread her, but then the memory of her matching him kiss for kiss told him otherwise.

Perhaps she was just as confused as he was about the kiss. What was going on between them? Was it something he wanted?

Ari didn't think so. He wasn't ready for the complications of a relationship. He wasn't over April, and he didn't think he could ever love another woman as much as he had loved his late wife. The last thing he wanted to do was hurt Natasha.

He had no right to kiss her like that, because he could never offer her his heart. There just wasn't enough room for two women. April had owned his heart completely.

"So will the consultant be meeting us for dinner?" Sage asked him. "I can't wait to meet Miss LeBlanc. I can usually get a good read on a person within five minutes."

"That's precisely why I wanted her to meet you," Ari said. His sister had an uncanny ability to really see inside a person. "But she has other plans tonight. However, you'll get to meet on Monday. We're going to have lunch together."

"Tell me about this woman," Blaze said with a grin. "Is she pretty?"

"What does that have to do with anything?" Sage wanted to know. "I don't care what she looks like. We just need to know if we can trust her."

"I'm just asking."

"Cut it out, you two," Ari said. "I need to

go over some stuff with you. Dad has a to-do list for all of us."

"Already? We just got here," Sage argued.

"You have met our dad, haven't you?" Ari asked. "We will work harder for him than any other employer in life."

She folded her arms across her chest. "So you're saying that Dad is a slave driver, in other words."

"I didn't say that, but yeah."

Sighing loudly, Sage pulled out her iPhone and a notepad from her tote. "I'm ready."

Ari and Blaze exchanged amused looks.

CHAPTER 14

Natasha didn't really have plans for the evening. She was just not ready to meet other members of the Alexander family. It was hard enough having to face Ari almost every day.

She regretted ever aligning herself with Harold, but there was nothing she could do about it now. For a brief second she considered going to Ari and confessing everything. Of course, she would lose any chance of receiving the money from Harold. Joshua deserved every opportunity to receive treatments for his leukemia.

Joshua didn't qualify for medical assistance because she made too much money, and Natasha couldn't get additional medical benefits because of his preexisting condition.

Tears filled her eyes. This was all such a mess right now.

"I just want to take care of my child," she

whispered. The fact was that if Joshua didn't get the treatments, he could die. "I can't lose my son."

Joshua came down the stairs and rushed over to her. "Mommy, can we watch a movie?"

"We sure can," she said as cheerfully as she could.

As much as she detested Harold DePaul, he was helping to keep her son alive. For that reason alone, he deserved her loyalty.

Natasha vowed to do what Harold wanted, and after that, she would be free of him. Besides, Malcolm was not a fool and he would never agree to take the company public. But she had done as Harold wanted, and he would have to keep his end of the bargain.

A wave of apprehension rose within.

What would happen to Joshua if Harold changed his mind and reneged on the payment?

Natasha didn't want to consider the alternative.

Ari enjoyed spending time with Blaze and Sage. They always had a good time together. The three of them had just finished watching a movie.

"So is that dude always around?" Sage

asked in a low voice. "He's creeping me out."

"He was our grandfather's butler," Ari explained. "His name is Franklin. He will be taking care of the house in Pacific Palisades. I'll take you there tomorrow."

"So, what are we going to do with him?" Blaze wanted to know. "We're not exactly the butler-type family."

Ari nodded in agreement. "Dad wasn't sure what to do about him. He was with Robert a long time. He finally decided to put him in charge of the staff."

Sage glanced over her shoulder. "Doesn't he ever go home?"

"He was living in the staff quarters here, but he's moving into one of the guesthouses on the estate in Pacific Palisades." Ari explained. "He was homeless when Robert met him."

"Wow . . ." Sage shook her head sadly. "Robert did a really nice thing. Wait a minute . . . did you say estate? We have an estate?"

Blaze and Ari laughed.

"If Mom and Dad don't want the chef, then I'll take him," Sage said. "I can't cook tap water."

"That's for sure," Blaze interjected.

She gave him a playful punch on the arm.

"I didn't ask you to cosign."

"Hey, you can't cook, Sage," Ari stated. "We all know that about you."

Blaze glanced around the residence. "I still can't get over this. Dad is Robert DePaul's biological son. Man, that's wild."

Ari nodded in understanding. "I just wish the DePaul family would stop trying to make him out to be a scam artist. Dad had nothing to do with any of this."

"I don't think anyone actually believes the claims those people are making," Sage interjected. "They know that the DePaul family is bitter because all of the money went to a black man. Nobody wants to say it, but this is why they are so upset."

"I don't know," Ari responded. "I think they'd be upset no matter what."

That evening, before he went to bed, Ari called Natasha.

"You didn't sound like yourself earlier, so I just wanted to make sure you were okay."

"I'm fine, Ari. Just wanted to take care of a few projects with deadlines and I wanted to spend some quality time with my son."

"Okay," he said. "I was concerned so I thought I'd call you back."

"I appreciate your concern, but I'm fine." She paused a moment before asking, "Are you enjoying your siblings?"

"I'm glad they're finally here. Now I can share the workload."

"Make sure you're getting in some downtime. I've noticed that you're a bit of a workaholic."

"I'm not doing much tomorrow. I'm taking Blaze and Sage to the house in Pacific Palisades. We will probably spend most of the day at the beach."

"Good for you," she said. "I'm so envious because I have to finish some work that's due next week, but I will be making up for it next weekend."

"You sound sleepy, so I'll let you go," Ari said. "Good night, Natasha."

"Have fun at the beach, and I'll see you on Monday."

When he hung up, Ari felt the hairs on the back of his neck stand up. He turned around to find Sage standing in the doorway, a mischievous grin on her face.

"Eh, did you need something?" he asked.

"Just wanted to say good-night." She blew him a kiss and disappeared.

Ari wondered how much of his conversation had been overheard by his sister. But mostly he was curious about the grin on her face. *What did she know? Does she have an inkling of my feelings for Natasha?*

He was going to have to be careful around

Sage. He wasn't ready to acknowledge his attraction to Natasha.

Monday morning, Ari drove his brother and sister over to the corporate offices.

"Is this another building we own?" Sage asked as they stepped into the lobby. "This is beautiful."

"Dad owns it," Ari corrected.

Natasha arrived within minutes of them.

Ari introduced her to Blaze and Sage.

Blaze shook her hand, saying, "I had no idea Los Angeles was filled with so many beautiful women."

"Thank you for the compliment," Natasha murmured.

He's flirting with her, Ari thought to himself, as he felt a tiny prick of betrayal. He sent a warning glare to Blaze.

Natasha shook Sage's hand next.

"Blaze, your office is across the hall," Ari said. "Why don't you head up to human resources and finalize your paperwork?" he suggested.

"I'll go with you," Sage said. "I'm sure I need to sign off on something."

"You and Blaze look like you can be twins."

"We're not," Ari said. "I'm two years older than him."

"Well, you two look alike."

"I'm the better-looking brother," Blaze interjected from behind them.

Jealously snaked down his spine the moment Ari caught his brother eyeing Natasha. Ari pulled Blaze aside.

"She's off-limits to you," he told him.

Blaze gave him a sidelong glance. "On whose orders?"

Ari walked away to get some air. When he returned, he found Blaze and Natasha in his office talking.

"Blaze, why don't you go back over to the hotel," he said. "You should discuss some of the promotional ideas you have with the marketing team there."

"I have a meeting scheduled with them later this afternoon."

"We're supposed to go to Santa Barbara. Did you forget?" Ari asked.

Sage glanced from one brother to the other. "What's going on between you two? I haven't seen you two argue like this since high school."

Blaze looked as puzzled as she did. "Nothing, as far as I know." He glanced in Ari's direction and asked, "Is there a problem?"

Ari pulled Blaze away from the others. "Stop flirting with Natasha."

"Excuse me?"

"You heard me," Ari responded. "We're supposed to be working, in case you've forgotten."

"Man, calm down," Blaze uttered. "Not everyone is always as serious as you are, Ari. Some of us like to laugh."

"Blaze, you know what Ari has been through," Sage interjected. "How could you say something like that to him?"

"It's time for Ari do something other than work all the time. I know how you feel, losing your wife like that —"

"How could you possibly know what that feels like, Blaze?" Ari asked, cutting him off. "What could you know of losing the only woman you've ever really loved?"

Blaze didn't respond.

Ari glanced over his shoulder. Natasha was standing a few feet away. The expression on her face confirmed his suspicion that she had heard everything.

She turned around and walked in the other direction.

"Dad would have a fit if he knew you two were acting this way," Sage told them in a low voice. "And don't forget, we're under a lot of scrutiny here, so get it together."

"Sage is right," Ari acknowledged. "I'm sorry, Blaze."

"Hey, me, too."

Ari went into his office and closed the door.

A few minutes later, there was a knock on the door.

"Come in," he said, expecting his visitor to be Natasha.

It was Tammie. She walked inside and closed the door behind her.

Ari hid his disappointment. "What can I do for you?"

She held up a folder and said, "I have the information you asked me to locate."

He smiled. "Great. Have a seat."

CHAPTER 15

Natasha was about to seek out Ari when she saw Tammie at his door. She was stunned when the young woman closed the door to the office.

The only time Ari's door was closed was when they were on conference calls or discussing something sensitive. What could Ari be discussing with Tammie behind closed doors? Tammie worked for supply management, but she reported to William DePaul. However, William was still at home recuperating.

She didn't want to admit that she was feeling a bit jealous. Tammie was a beautiful young woman, after all.

Natasha chided herself for the way she was feeling.

She went into the conference room to make a phone call to her assistant.

Sage found her there a few minutes later.

"How are things going?" Natasha inquired.

"Fine," Sage responded as she sat down in one of the empty chairs. "I'm going back to the hotel with Blaze so that I can tour each of the residences. I want photos and a thorough one-sheet with all of the features."

Natasha leaned forward and asked, "Is Ari upset with me?"

Sage gave her a reassuring smile. "Natasha, my brother is a very intense man at times. After working with him for a few weeks, you'll learn his moods."

Natasha nodded. "How are you enjoying Los Angeles?"

"I love it so far," Sage responded, "but it does take some getting used to all the traffic, however."

"Yeah," Natasha said in agreement. "It will soon become second nature to you."

They heard Ari's voice as he was walking down the hallway and their conversation changed.

"Robert's vision for the residences was to elevate everyday living," Natasha told Sage. "He wanted the owners to feel transformed as they stepped off the private elevator into the elegance of their own luxury home."

Sage jotted down notes as she talked. "I like that. We should make it part of the press release and marketing material."

"Sounds like you two are busy," Ari said.

"I wanted to let you know that I have to step out of the office for a couple of hours."

Sage and Natasha exchanged puzzled looks.

"Where are you going?" his sister asked.

Natasha wondered the same but didn't dare question him in front of Sage.

"I have to meet with someone," was all Ari said.

He left the conference room, walking briskly.

"Must be important," Sage murmured.

"Yeah," Natasha agreed. This wasn't the first time Ari had acted so secretly. There was something going on, and Malcolm was in on it.

Natasha and Ari spent the rest of the week in a flurry of meetings, fielding requests for interviews and reassuring the employees. She missed the easy conversations they used to have. Natasha also noted how Ari had warned his brother to stay away from her.

Now there seemed to be all this tension between them. Ari was also more close-mouthed than usual whenever it came to certain company information. Did he suspect something between her and Harold? How could he have found out?

She and Sage had become instant friends,

however. It seemed they spent more time together than she and Ari.

Natasha took a deep breath then exhaled slowly. She made her way to Ari's office and knocked on the door that stood slightly ajar. "May I come in?" she asked.

"Of course," he responded.

"Ari, have I done something to offend you?"

Confused, Ari asked, "Why would you think that, Natasha?"

"There seems to be some tension between us. It wasn't there before."

"I'm sorry," he said. "There's been a lot going on, as you well know, but I haven't meant to push you to the side. Let me make it up to you. Have dinner with me, if you have no other plans. We'll make it an early one because I know you want to get home to your son."

She broke into a smile. "I'd love to have dinner with you."

"I have to be over at the hotel around three, so why don't you meet me over there at five. We can talk while we eat."

She rose to her feet. "I'll see you at five."

Natasha left the office feeling better about her relationship with Ari. She was glad they would get a chance to talk.

"Is my brother in his office?" Sage asked

when she ran into Natasha in the hallway.

"Yes," Natasha responded. "I just left there."

"Are things better between you two?" Sage wanted to know.

"We're having dinner this evening," she said. "I think we'll soon be back on track. At least I hope so."

"Well, I need to speak to him before he leaves, so I'll give you a call later this evening."

"I'm leaving in a few," Natasha announced. "I have a staff meeting."

She stopped to gather her purse and tote then headed out to the parking lot. She would be working from her own office for the rest of the day.

Four hours later, Natasha pulled up to the entrance of the Alexander-DePaul Beverly Hills Hotel & Spa Resort. She handed her keys to the valet and rushed inside. She was ten minutes late for her dinner date with Ari.

He was seated at one of the tables near the back of the restaurant.

"I was worried that you'd changed your mind about having dinner with me."

Natasha shook her head. "I've been looking forward to this all day. I've really missed our conversations."

He met her gaze. "So have I."

After they placed their order, Natasha handed her menu to the waiter. "You look tired, Ari."

"I am," he confessed. "William will be back on Monday and my parents will be here at the end of June, so I expect my workload will be even lighter."

Natasha was surprised. "William DePaul is staying on?" Harold had told her that William would be leaving.

"Yeah, he and my dad talked. He was never in agreement with the way his family reacted to Robert's will."

Natasha had been told otherwise by Harold. She should've known better than to believe him.

"Hey, why the frown?" Ari asked.

She pasted a smile on her face. "I'm sorry. I was just shocked by the news of William's return. I thought he would follow Harold."

"I thought so, too," Ari said. "But apparently, the two don't get along well." He reached for his wine glass. "Enough about them. When am I going to see your skills on the basketball court?"

"How about this weekend?" Natasha asked. "I'm playing a game with some of my old teammates. It's for charity. You can invite Blaze and your sister, too."

"How about I come alone?"

She swallowed her surprise. "Sure. That would be okay, too."

Their food arrived.

"I think we need to talk about what happened between us," Ari blurted. "We need to discuss that kiss and what it meant."

Natasha nodded. "Is this why you've been so distant with me?"

"I never should've crossed that line with you."

"Ari, I'm not your employee. I'm also not going to sue you for sexual harassment. I enjoyed that kiss as much as you did. My only question is, why did you kiss me in the first place?"

"I am very attracted to you," Ari confessed. "But we work together."

Natasha wiped her mouth on the end of her napkin. "I like you, Ari, and I enjoy your company."

"So you just want to be friends? Is that what you're saying?"

"I'm saying that we don't have to put a label on anything," Natasha explained. "I know that you are still grieving your wife and that you haven't dated anyone since her death. Why don't we try being friends first?"

Ari's smile warmed her. "I'd like that very much."

Ari was in the kitchen when Blaze walked in.

"How was your date with Natasha?" he inquired.

"It wasn't a date," Ari retorted.

"Call it whatever makes you feel better, but the truth is that you have feelings for that woman, Ari." Blaze poured himself a glass of orange juice.

"I don't know if I'll ever be ready for another relationship," Ari confessed. "It hurt too much losing April. I can't go through another loss like that."

"So you're just going to give up on love?"

"I'm not in love."

"Ari, you bite my head off every time I speak to Natasha." Blaze met his brother's gaze. "You're falling for her."

"We are getting to know one another — that's what people do when they work together, Blaze."

"It's more than that, big brotha."

Ari didn't confirm or deny. Instead, he focused on his cooking. He didn't want to overcook the scrambled eggs.

"April doesn't want you to spend the rest of your life alone," Blaze stated. "You know that's not what she wanted for you."

"Blaze, I'm fine. Right now, I have enough on my plate with the company."

"Ari, that company won't keep you warm at night. Just remember that."

"Why don't we table the matchmaking for a later time?" Ari suggested. "We've got a lot of work ahead of us, so let's focus."

"Have you even told Natasha that you're interested in her?" Blaze inquired.

Ari stole a peek over his shoulder. "Will you drop all the matchmaking?"

"I'm just saying."

"Then stop it," Ari snapped out of frustration. "I am here to focus on the job. You know, it would help tremendously if you and I were on the same page."

Blaze broke into a grin. "Whatever you say, big brotha."

Ari hated being so transparent. He hoped that Blaze would keep his mouth shut while Ari tried to sort out his feelings. Since meeting Natasha, he had been torn by conflicting emotions. Ari was glad his parents were finally making the move to California on Saturday. Once his father arrived, Natasha would be spending most of her time with Malcolm.

They needed some distance between them. Ari tried to rationalize that his feelings were because it had been three years since he'd been with a woman. The last year of April's life was spent battling the cancer. She had been so sick; Ari didn't pressure her for sex. Although they couldn't make love, the intimacy between them continued.

He was a man and he loved sex, but what Ari desired most went much deeper than lust. He wanted a heart connection. He had had that with April. Surely, no man could find that kind of love twice in a lifetime.

Natasha definitely had skills when it came to playing basketball. So did her sister, who was in town to play. He sat with Natalie's fiancé and Joshua.

"My mommy's very good at basketball," the little boy told Ari. "She's a point guard."

"I see," he responded.

"She has skills. My auntie Natalie does, too."

Again, Ari agreed.

He studied the little boy, noting the faint circles beneath his eyes, the shaved head and how frail he looked. Natasha had never mentioned that her son was sick. He never once heard her complain about anything, he thought with a renewed respect for her.

After the game, they all went to a nearby restaurant for dinner.

"Mr. Ari, do you have any children?" Joshua asked.

"I'm afraid I don't," he replied. "Not yet, anyway."

"I would like a brother or sister," he announced, soliciting laughter from his aunt and her fiancé.

"Mr. Ari, can I tell you a secret?" Joshua asked in a whisper.

"Sure." He leaned down, putting his ear close to the boy's mouth.

"I have leukemia, but Mommy says we are going to beat it. I don't like the treatments. They make me really sick."

Stunned, Ari glanced over at Natasha, who was watching them.

He turned his attention back to Joshua and said, "I think you are a very brave boy and your mother's right. You will beat this."

Natasha had never once mentioned that her son was battling leukemia. There was no reason why she should've confided in him. He admired her strength and courage.

Later that evening, she called him at home.

"I'm sorry you had to find out about Joshua that way," Natasha told him. "I hadn't planned to tell you until I had gotten to know you better. It's just not something you blurt out."

"I understand," he said.

"The other reason is because I don't like giving voice to it. My son is going to be healed from this disease. I have to believe it, and by saying that he has it . . . well, I would rather say that he is cancer free."

"I know what you mean," Ari told her. "April had breast cancer, but by the time we found out, she was stage four. There wasn't anything that could be done."

"You didn't give up on her, did you?" Natasha asked in a small voice.

"No, I didn't. She didn't give up, either. We fought until the very end."

He could tell Natasha was crying.

"Honey, your son is going to grow up to be big and strong," he said, wanting to reassure her. "They have made some wonderful strides in medicine."

"I know," Natasha murmured. "I have to be so strong for Joshua and for my parents. Sometimes, I just need to cry. It's not that I'm doubting his healing. *I'm not.*"

"Natasha, I am here if you ever need me," Ari promised. "Call me anytime, day or night. You do not have to go through this alone."

"Thank you," she murmured softly.

"Are you okay?" he asked.

"Not really," Natasha confessed. "I feel

really alone. My sister and her fiancé are here, but . . ."

His feelings for her were intensifying, and the thought of her hurting bothered Ari. "Would you like some company?"

"Yes."

"Give me your address and I'll be on my way."

Ten minutes later, Ari was in his car and driving away from the hotel.

Natasha opened the door to let Ari inside.

They stood staring at one another with longing. There was no denying that they shared an intense physical awareness of each other.

Without warning, Ari pulled her into his arms, kissing her. He held her snugly in his arms.

A brief shiver rippled through Natasha. She buried her face against the corded muscles of his chest. She had no desire to back out of his embrace.

"I'm so glad you're here."

He gazed down at her with tenderness. "I will be here for as long as you need me."

Parting her lips, she raised herself to meet his kiss. His lips pressed against hers then gently covered her mouth. The kiss sent the pit of Natasha's stomach into a wild swirl.

Ari showered her with kisses around her lips and along her jaw. As he roused her passion, his own grew stronger.

This time, it was Natasha who slowly pulled away. She took him by the hand and led him over to the sofa.

"I don't know why I became so needy," she said as she sat down beside him. "I'm not usually like this, Ari."

"You're not a robot, sweetheart," he whispered, stroking her hair. "At some point, you will break down emotionally. I know this from experience."

Natasha settled back, enjoying the feel of his arms around her. "My sister is getting married in a couple of months and my brother has a very happy marriage — it just reminds me of how much I'm lacking when it comes to love. I get lonely sometimes."

"So do I," Ari confessed. "I use work to take my mind off of just how lonely I feel."

His closeness was so male, so bracing.

He stroked her cheek. "What are you thinking about?"

"You want the truth?" she asked.

Ari nodded.

"I was thinking about how long it's been since I've been this close to a man. How long it's been since I've kissed a man or made love." She raised her eyes to meet his.

"It's been a while."

"Same here," Ari murmured.

"I'm not trying to seduce you," Natasha interjected quickly. "Ari, I'm sure you are aware that I'm attracted to you. I know that you're dealing with a lot right now, and so am I. I meant what I said about us being friends."

He seemed to relax a little.

"Sweetheart, I'm attracted to you, too. But I have to be honest. It almost feels as if I'm cheating on April."

"You haven't made peace with her death," Natasha said.

"I guess I haven't," Ari responded. "It wouldn't be fair to drag you into my mess right now. Natasha, if you could be patient with me — I'd like to see where this goes."

His words surprised her. "What exactly are you saying to me?"

"I just want to take whatever this is between us one day at a time."

Smiling, Natasha nodded in agreement. "I feel the same way. If and when we do make love, I don't want a ghost in the room."

Her words were met with silence.

Ari checked his watch and rose to his feet. "It's getting late."

She stood up. "Thank you for coming, Ari."

"I want you to know that I heard what you said and I respect that. If our relationship takes off in that direction, I want to give myself to you completely and without guilt." He brushed a gentle kiss across her forehead. "Good night, sweetheart."

Ari quietly made his way to the door and eased it open. "Oh, you do have skills on the court. We'll have to play one weekend. Won't be much of a game on your end, I'm just saying."

"Talk is cheap," she whispered.

He was gone, but even in remembrance Natasha felt the intimacy of his kisses.

She went to her bedroom and got ready for bed.

The soft knock on her door startled her.

Natalie stuck her head inside and asked, "What's up with you and Ari?" She walked in and sat down on her sister's bed. "I saw you two out there kissing up a storm."

"I don't know yet," she responded with a smile. "He isn't over his deceased wife. He still wears his wedding ring."

"That may be true, but sis, he seems to care a great deal for you," Natalie stated. "And watching him with Joshua . . . I think it was love at first sight for those two."

"Ari loves children."

"Well, I like him, sis. I don't see any

reason why you two can't be together." Natalie stretched and yawned. "I'll see you in the morning."

Natasha knew of one reason why she and Ari could never be truly happy. *Harold DePaul.*

Sage also had the same question the next day while they were having lunch.

"Natasha, you can tell me to mind my own business, but I have to ask — are you interested in Ari?"

"W-why would you ask me something like that?"

"I've seen the way you two look at each other when you think no one is watching. There's something you should know about my brother," Sage was saying. "Ari has only been involved with one woman his entire life. When she died, I was worried that we would lose him, too. I've never seen so much grief."

"He loves her with his entire being."

"Body and soul," Sage murmured. "But now that he's met you, I think he's ready to move on with his life, but you may have to be the one to take the relationship to the next level."

"I'm not sure what you mean."

"You have to be honest and up-front with Ari about your feelings for him, because my dear brother may not have a clue."

Natasha shook her head. "I don't think I can do that, Sage. Ari and I have decided to build our friendship." She thought back to her conversation last night with Ari. "He has to find closure with his wife's death. Until then, we won't have any type of future."

"He told me about Joshua," Sage blurted. "Please don't get mad at him."

"I'm not. It wasn't a secret or anything. I just don't go around announcing that my son has leukemia."

Sage checked her iPhone. "Ari just sent me a text. He wants us to meet him and Blaze at the hotel in Pacific Palisades."

They finished their lunch and then headed out to the car.

"There are no residences at this hotel, right?" Sage inquired.

"Right," Natasha replied. "It's a very nice hotel, but it caters to more of the spa crowd. It's not quite as grand as the one in Beverly Hills, but it's still five-star quality."

Natasha hadn't seen Ari at all since last night. She and Sage had been together most of the morning at the Beverly Hills property going over appraisal reports.

"Have you decided which unit you're going to move into?" Natasha asked once they settled inside the limo.

"I think the one across from Ari's. It's the smallest unit we have, but it's perfect for me. Two bedrooms are really all I need for now."

An image of Ari and Joshua together formed in Natasha's mind, placing a smile on her face. Since meeting Ari, Joshua couldn't stop talking about the man.

Chapter 16

Ari and Blaze took the elevator to the executive suite.

Tastefully painted walls with warm walnut wood trim, accompanied by a spectacular view of a lush botanical garden greeted them.

Ari eyed the appetizing presentation of delicacies for them to enjoy during their meeting.

"I don't know which one I like better," Blaze said. "This one or the one in Beverly Hills."

"They are both beautiful and well-appointed," Ari responded. His eyes traveled the room and landed on the sunken full-service bar with seating for eight.

Blaze picked up what looked like a remote control. "Oh, look at this," he murmured. "It's for the drapes." He put it down and ventured over to the fifty-inch plasma TV and home-theater system with surround sound.

"As you can see, all of our suites have been designed to feel more like an opulent residence than a temporary getaway," Tom White, the general manager, said as they toured the penthouse suite.

He took them to see the presidential suite.

"How big is this suite?" Blaze asked.

"It's four thousand square feet. In this suite, our guests can enjoy a private solarium, indoor garden and fountain. There are two master bedrooms with steam showers, whirlpool tubs and a conference room. If they require rooms for personal staff, there are three one-thousand-square foot entourage suites available on this same floor.

"This was Mr. DePaul's personal suite," Tom announced when they walked to the end of the hall. "It now belongs to your family."

Ari noted the room was similar to the presidential suite.

"Is it four thousand square feet, as well?" Blaze inquired.

"Yes, it is. Should you require any additional rooms, please let us know and we will accommodate all of you."

The amenities matched those in the presidential suite.

On Ari's left was a formal dining room for twelve behind floor-to-ceiling glass doors.

He strode over to the office and peeked inside.

"Gramps really knew how to live, didn't he?" Blaze commented. "I wonder what Mom and Dad are going to think when they see everything they own."

"It's overwhelming," Ari stated.

"Have you considered what I said?" Blaze asked.

Ari gave a stiff nod. "Nothing's changed. If I even think about another woman, I am filled with guilt. It's like I'm cheating on April."

"But you're not."

"I know that in my head, but try telling that to my heart."

"If you don't make a move quick, you may end up losing Natasha for good," Blaze advised. "She's a gorgeous woman. She's not going to sit around and wait for you forever."

Ari didn't respond.

He had feelings for Natasha, but he didn't know what to do about them. Ari was still very much in love with April, even though she was gone. He wasn't sure another woman could ever take her place — there just wasn't enough room in his heart. There was also Joshua to consider. Ari had faith that the little boy would beat leukemia, but the thought of dealing with cancer a second time . . . he had a lot to consider.

As soon as they arrived to the hotel, Ari pulled Natasha off to the side and said, "I'd like to visit the properties in Northern California over the next couple of weeks. Do you have anything pressing on your schedule?"

"No, I can go with you, but I'll need to fly home in the evenings to be with Joshua. I don't like spending my nights away from home."

"We can discuss this further, but not right now. We were just about to tour the spa and salon," Ari announced. "You two are just in time."

Tom held the door open for them. "Our guests can select from therapeutic facial and body treatments, massage therapies and enjoy our state-of-the art fitness facility."

Sage broke into a smile. "You know, I'm feeling like I need some rejuvenation."

"Not this trip," Ari said. "You're supposed to be working."

"Why don't you get a massage, Ari?" Sage suggested. "Maybe it'll help lighten you up some."

Blaze and Natasha stifled their chuckles.

Ari sent them a hard glare, which silenced them.

After the tour, Ari and Natasha sat down at a table in the café. "By the way, I was thinking that Sage and Blaze should travel with us."

Natasha nodded in approval. "Is it okay with you if I fly home in the evenings? If not, then I won't be able to go with you all."

"Why don't you consider bringing Joshua with us?" Ari suggested. "You can bring along your babysitter, nanny or whoever you have watching him."

Natasha was clearly touched by his consideration. "Ari, I think that would actually be wonderful. Are you sure that you don't mind?"

"Not at all."

They were joined by Blaze and Sage.

"I'm glad I have all of you here," Natasha said. "Ari has made it clear what he thinks about a formal gala to introduce your family to Beverly Hills."

Sage and Blaze exchanged looks.

"What?" Natasha glanced from one to the other.

"We aren't really the gala type of family, Natasha," Sage said after a moment. "The only time we really get dressed up like that is when we're attending a charity fundraiser or a wedding."

Natasha gazed at Ari. "You're enjoying this, aren't you?"

"I tried to tell you," he responded.

"What about you, Blaze? What are your thoughts on this?"

"I agree with Sage," he replied. "I think a barbecue is more our style."

She shook her head. "Ari said the same thing. You guys are definitely related. But as I explained to your brother, a large formal affair is more suited to Beverly Hills."

"But it's not us," Sage countered. "If we're introducing our family to everyone, then don't you think they should get a real sense of who we truly are? An expensive gala in designer gowns, gourmet foods and tuxedos do not reflect the Alexander family."

Blaze nodded in agreement.

Natasha sighed in resignation. "Okay, I give up."

"Mom and Dad have the final say, but I'm pretty sure they will prefer a barbecue."

"Ari, are you busy tonight?" Natasha blurted before she lost her nerve. They had just returned to the hotel in Beverly Hills.

"No, what's up?"

"Would you like to have dinner with me

and Joshua?" She grinned. "You're not the only one with skills in the kitchen."

"I'd love to join you for dinner."

"How does eight o'clock sound?"

"Perfect."

"What's perfect?" Sage asked, walking over to where they were standing.

"Natasha and I were having a *private* conversation."

Sage gave him a sly smile. "Well, I guess I'll be going then. I'll give you a call later, Natasha."

Ari laughed as his sister sashayed away. "She doesn't have a subtle bone in her body."

"I need to get out of here, Ari. I have to stop by the store on the way home so that I can cook you a fabulous dinner."

"I'm in the mood for fabulous."

She smiled at him. "Good."

Ari walked her out to her car. "I'll see you in a couple of hours."

In a surprise move, he kissed her.

When he released Natasha, he said, "There is no wine this time."

She pulled his head down to hers, covering his lips with hers. "I've wanted to do this all day."

Ari's feelings for Natasha and the guilt that plagued him had nothing to do with reason. Yet, he couldn't shake the feeling that he was being unfaithful to April. He had been faithful to her in all the years they were together. It was time to move on, but Ari didn't know how.

Malcolm and Barbara Alexander arrived Saturday afternoon. Natasha, Ari and his siblings, along with the staff, greeted them when they walked into the hotel.

Ari introduced Natasha to his mother.

"It's a pleasure to finally meet you," Barbara said. "I've heard a lot about you."

Natasha smiled. "All good, I hope."

Members of the staff came up to say hello and introduce themselves.

"I'm sorry about having you give up part of your Saturday like this," Ari said.

"Oh, this is fine. I wanted to meet your mother." Natasha glanced over to where Malcolm and Barbara were standing. "They are so patient. I'm sure they can't wait to get to the penthouse."

"They will stay down here as long as needed," Ari told her. "My parents really appreciate their employees."

She looked up at him. "I guess this means we won't be working together as much."

Initially, Ari had wanted to put distance between them, but now, he dreaded the thought. "Dad okayed the tour to see the rest of the properties. He also said you can take your son and the nanny."

"She's actually his nurse," Natasha corrected. "That's great. Joshua is going to be so excited."

His parents navigated to the private elevator, retreating to the penthouse to relax from their early morning travel.

"I guess I'll see you on Monday," Ari told Natasha. "I don't want to take up all of your day."

"I promised Joshua that I'd take him to the movies, so I better get out of here."

Ari didn't want her to leave, but he remained silent. Weekends were quality time for Natasha and Joshua. He would not be selfish by keeping her away from her son. Joshua needed her.

The following week, they took the private plane to San Francisco. With his parents at the helm, this was the perfect time to see the other properties.

Sage and Natasha sat and talked with Monica. Joshua and Ari sat together so that they could play a game.

Blaze sat alone behind them, eyes closed and earphones attached to his iPhone.

Every now and then, he bobbed his head

as if listening to music.

They landed an hour later.

They were ushered to a limo, which drove them to the Alexander-DePaul San Francisco Hotel & Spa Resort.

"Blaze and I are going to fly back to Los Angeles tonight," Sage announced. "Dad needs us to take care of some stuff for him."

Natasha stole a peek at Ari, trying to read his expression.

He shrugged and said, "Well, it looks like it's just going to be you and me, Natasha."

"I suppose we'll have to find a way to manage without them."

Ari broke into a grin. "I'm up to the challenge. How about you?"

Natasha nodded.

"I get the feeling we're not going to be missed at all," Blaze said.

Sage winked at Natasha and replied, "Me, too."

As soon as they arrived to the hotel, Natasha checked Monica and Joshua into their suite. Once she had them settled, she went downstairs to join the others, who were in a conference with the general manager.

"This hotel is nestled in the heart of this amazing city, but miles away from an ordinary experience. We recently completed renovation and now feature five hundred guest rooms and suites," the manager was saying.

Natasha sat down beside Sage.

After their meeting, they were taken on a tour to see the newly renovated guest rooms and suites.

"You and Blaze really don't have to leave," Natasha told Sage in a low whisper. "To be honest, I think Ari is more comfortable having you two here with us."

Sage shook her head. "Trust me. My brother wants to have you all to himself."

"Did he tell you this?"

"Not in so many words," Sage responded. "But I know how he thinks."

"I don't know about this."

"You and Ari need some time alone."

"Sage, we are not in a relationship. Your brother and I are just friends."

"Not yet, but who knows what will happen this week."

CHAPTER 17

Ari cornered his brother outside a conference room and asked, "Okay, tell me the truth. Why are you and Sage really leaving?"

"Dad wants us back in Beverly Hills. He has some marketing ideas he wants to run by me, and he wants to go over some development projects with Sage."

"That's interesting," Ari murmured. "I just got off the phone with Dad and he told me that *you* called him and said that you and Sage would be returning home this evening. What's up, Blaze?"

"We just thought that you and Natasha could use some time alone," Blaze responded with a grin. "But we hadn't counted on her bringing Joshua and the nanny."

Frowning, Ari stated, "This is a business trip. You and Sage need to learn about each of these hotels. Especially you, Blaze."

"I will be traveling to see all of the hotels

over the next month, so don't worry about me. I know how to do my job." Blaze paused a moment before adding, "It's okay for you to move on, Ari. April wouldn't hold it against you if you fell in love with another woman."

"No, she wouldn't," Ari agreed. "But I don't know if that woman is Natasha Le-Blanc."

"Then why not find out for sure?" Blaze queried. "You will never know if you don't take a chance."

"From the moment I looked into those gorgeous brown eyes of hers — it's like I'm on drugs. I can't get enough of looking at her."

"I have a strong suspicion that she feels the same way about you."

Ari met his brother's gaze. "Are we really that transparent?"

Blaze nodded. "Use this time together to explore your feelings for one another."

"It's been a long time since I felt this way about a woman."

"In my opinion, it's long overdue," Blaze responded. "Don't get me wrong. You know that I loved April like a sister, but it really hurt me to see you grieve so much."

"I miss her so much. She was my best friend."

Blaze nodded in understanding. "I miss her, too. But the thing is . . . Ari, you need to start living again."

"I'm not sure I know how," Ari confessed.

"She's a start."

He followed Blaze's line of vision and nodded.

"Why don't we get in the limo and take Joshua sightseeing?" Ari suggested after Blaze and Sage left to fly back to Los Angeles.

"I've never been here before, so I'd like to see some of the city. I figured Joshua might like to get out of the suite. Plus, it will give Monica some time to herself."

Natasha considered his idea. "Joshua will be thrilled, but I want to make sure he's feeling okay and doesn't have a fever."

They sat down in the lobby.

"Joshua was a typical five-year-old boy, Ari. He loved playing football, wrestling and playing with his friends. Around Thanksgiving, I noticed he was tiring and started to run a low-grade fever. I also noticed he was starting to bruise easily when he bumped into things. I took him to the pediatrician, who ran a blood test. I found out on Christmas Eve that Joshua had leukemia."

Ari reached over, taking Natasha by the hand.

"I know that he's going to be fine," she said. "But there are times when I get scared."

"Everything within me also tells me that Joshua is going to be fine."

She ran her fingers through her curls. "I believe it, also."

They sat there for a moment in silence.

"I guess I better get to the suite," Natasha said. "Joshua is probably wondering where I am."

"Should I reserve the limo?"

"Sure. I'll call you in a few minutes."

Ari watched her leave before walking over to the concierge desk. "What can I do for you, Mr. Alexander?"

"I need you to arrange something for me." Ari told him exactly what he had in mind."

"I can arrange everything for you, Mr. Alexander."

He left there and made his way to the private elevator that would take him to the penthouse suite.

Ari quickly changed into a pair of jeans and a polo shirt.

"We'll meet you in the lobby," Natasha told him when she called. "Joshua's so excited."

He left the penthouse ten minutes later.

Joshua was waiting near the elevator when he stepped out. "Mr. Ari, what took you so long?"

"I'm sorry," he said. "I didn't mean to make you wait."

Ari scooped Joshua up in his arms. "Let's go."

"C'mon, Mommy."

"I'm right behind you," she said.

"I like riding in this limo," Joshua told him. "I feel like I'm in a submarine."

Ari and Natasha laughed.

As soon as they returned to the hotel, Joshua had dinner and then went into the room to watch television. When Natasha checked on him, she found him asleep, holding on to the toy horse Ari bought him.

"Joshua had such a wonderful time today," Natasha commented. "Ari, thank you so much for everything you did for my son." She hadn't seen Joshua this excited about anything in a long time. Natasha's eyes teared up as she recalled how attentive Ari was with her little boy.

"He's a great kid and I wanted to make today special for him."

She pulled his face down to hers and kissed him.

Ari wrapped his arms around her, drawing her closer in his embrace. Her body pressed to his, he felt blood coursing through his veins like an awakened river.

Their eyes locked as their breathing came in unison.

Natasha tried to ignore the aching in her limbs and the pulsing knot that had formed in her stomach.

Without a word, Ari swept her, weightless, into his arms.

Inside the bedroom, he eased her down onto the bed. His hand unbuttoned her blouse, but before Ari could go any further, he pulled away, saying, "I'm sorry."

His rejection was like a bucket of cold water. It washed over her, cooling her ardor.

"It's okay," she said as she began buttoning up her top. "I understand."

But the truth was that Natasha didn't understand at all. Ari wanted her and she wanted him to make love to her. The ghost of his late wife was present. Her ex-husband never had problems sleeping with other women, despite their marriage. Ari was truly like no other man she'd ever met. She always seemed to meet men who couldn't stay faithful, but Ari was faithful to a fault.

Natasha looked up at him, noting his pain-filled gaze. "You're just not ready, Ari."

"You are such a beautiful woman. I . . ."

"It's okay," she said with a shrug. "Why don't we just keep this at friendship?"

"I'm sorry."

"Stop apologizing." Natasha eased off the bed. "Joshua might wake up at any moment."

He followed her out of the bedroom.

She walked him to the door. "Enjoy your evening, Ari."

"I —"

Natasha didn't want to hear another word. "It's best you just leave."

Ari felt like such a heel.

Natasha was right. It was best that they just remain friends. He never should have gotten involved with her on a personal level. He had vowed to never get involved with someone he was working with, but Natasha changed all that for him. From the moment he saw her, Ari knew that his life would never be the same.

"I should have kept it business between us," he whispered.

It was too late now.

Ari was in love with Natasha.

He had never thought he could love someone else. He had loved April with his heart and soul. But Natasha was able to infiltrate his heart, leaving Ari conflicted.

The next morning, Natasha left her room hoping to avoid Ari, but he was just leaving his suite.

"Good morning," she said, not looking at him.

"I'm sorry about last night."

She shrugged in nonchalance. "Forget about it. *I have.*" Natasha was not about to let him know how much his rejection hurt her.

Ari's eyebrows arched a fraction at her words. The air suddenly felt thick with tension between them.

He tried to make small talk while they were in the elevator, but Natasha didn't have much to say. She could no longer deny that she had fallen in love with Ari, but he was still in love with his dead wife.

She walked out of the elevator as soon as the doors opened. Ari quickened his pace to catch up with her. "We need to talk."

Natasha slowed her pace. "There's nothing else to be said, Ari. You've made yourself very clear. You are still very much in love with April."

Keeping his voice low, he responded, "Apparently, you're upset with me. We need to discuss this."

"No, I'm not, Ari," she snapped. "Look, let's just focus on why we're here."

"Natasha, I do care for you."

"I can't deal with this right now." Natasha glared at him. "Please, Ari. Let's just forget about last night."

"It's not that easy for me," he told her.

"Then it's your problem." She walked away from him as soon as she spotted the food and beverage manager.

Ari didn't follow her. He thought it was best to give her some time alone.

He spent most of his morning checking on some information Malcolm had requested regarding the renovations.

By lunchtime, Ari went looking for Natasha. He found her in the café with Samuel, the general manager. They looked pretty cozy, he thought jealously. When the man reached over and covered Natasha's hand with his own, Ari couldn't help but wonder if they had been involved in the past.

He returned to the office he was using for the day.

Natasha found him there half an hour later. "I just wanted to apologize for snapping at you. It was unprofessional of me."

"Apology accepted."

"Have you eaten anything today? Samuel

and I were expecting you to join us for lunch."

"I wasn't hungry. Besides, you and Samuel looked pretty cozy."

"Ari, what's wrong with you?" she asked.

"Could you close the door behind you, please?"

Natasha did as he requested. "I hope we are not about to rehash —"

He cut her off by blurting, "Were you involved with him?"

"With Samuel? Ari, he's a married man." She looked at Ari as if he'd grown three heads. "What type of woman do you think I am?"

"I saw you two in the café. He was practically all over you."

Natasha shook her head. "It wasn't like that." She couldn't believe he was jealous. He had some nerve, when he couldn't let go of his late wife.

"I stood there watching the two of you. I know what I saw."

"Then you should put on your glasses." She turned to leave.

"Natasha, please don't leave."

"Then don't go there with me, Ari," she warned.

"I'm just saying that the man is attracted to you."

She dismissed his words with a wave of her hand. "You are wrong on so many levels, Ari."

He gave her a knowing look. "Did he invite you to dinner?"

"He's just being nice. We are having dinner tonight, but you can join us if you're so concerned."

He shook his head. "He didn't invite me, so I'll be in the suite tonight contemplating his future with the company."

Her anger dissipated and Natasha broke into a grin. "You wouldn't."

Ari gave her a tiny smile. "Actually, I'll be having a great dinner in my suite with Joshua."

"You don't have to babysit for me."

"I'm not. Joshua and I have had this date already planned. Since Monica has some friends here in San Francisco, I thought it would be nice to give her some time off so that she can visit with them. And give you a break. I was going to suggest you go to the spa for a pampering session, but . . ."

"I won't be out late. It's an early dinner."

"It's fine," he assured her. "Have fun."

Natasha shook her head. "I can't do this."

"You can and you will. Joshua and I will have a good time together."

"Are you sure about this?"

He nodded.

"You don't look like you're okay with me having dinner with Samuel."

"No, it's fine," he assured her, but deep down, it bothered him that she was having dinner with another man.

Samuel leaned forward and said, "I'm glad to see I was wrong about you."

She frowned. "What are you talking about?"

"I thought you and Ari were involved, but if that were true, you certainly wouldn't be here with me right now."

Natasha took a sip of her iced tea.

"I was thinking that maybe we could spend some time together to get to know one another."

"Aren't you married?"

"My wife and I are not doing well. In fact, the only reason we are still together is because of our children. She does her thing and I do mine."

"Samuel, I have to be honest with you," she said. "I find that disgusting."

"Excuse me?"

"Either you're married or you're not," Natasha uttered. "Cheating is not the way to fix a troubled marriage."

"I told you that we are only together for

our children."

"It doesn't matter to me," she stated. "Thanks for dinner, but I've got to get upstairs to my son."

"Natasha, I didn't mean to upset you." He grabbed her hand, but she snatched it away. "I'm sorry."

"Samuel, we've known each other a long time. I've even thought of you as a friend. Don't ruin that for me."

He gave a stiff nod.

Natasha rose to her feet and then patted him on the shoulder. "Have a good evening, Samuel."

She hated having to admit that Ari had been right all along about Samuel.

"What's wrong?" Ari asked when she came to his suite.

"Ari, you were right."

He burst into laughter.

"It's not that funny." Natasha sat down on the sofa while Ari opted for one of the accent chairs.

"So what happened? He made a pass at you?"

"Yeah. I don't understand why men get married if they want to continue seeing other women."

"I'm afraid I don't have an answer for you, either."

"Enough about that jerk," she uttered. "Did you and Joshua have a good time?"

"We did," Ari confirmed. "Monica came to the suite and he fussed until she promised he could watch a Disney movie until he fell asleep. I checked on him fifteen minutes ago and he was sleeping. Natasha, you really have a great little boy."

"I think so."

"We made cards to give to the children at one of the hospitals here in San Francisco."

"Joshua loves doing that. He says that it makes him feel much better.

"What were you doing?" she asked, gesturing toward the stack of paperwork on the desk.

"Dad emailed me a laundry list of things to check on while we're here."

Natasha removed her purse from her shoulder. "Anything I can help with?"

"No, I have everything under control."

He seemed to be peering at her intently. Natasha saw the heart-rending tenderness of his gaze.

She rose to her feet. "I'll leave you to your work, then."

Natasha secretly hoped that he would ask her to stay awhile longer, but he didn't, much to her disappointment.

"I'll see you tomorrow morning."

She tried to swallow the lump lingering in her throat. She had fallen in love with a man who would never be able to return that love. The thought shattered her heart into a million little pieces.

CHAPTER 18

Ari tossed and turned in bed.

He was having a hard time sleeping. Finally, he gave up and got out of bed. He padded barefoot into the living room and sat down at the desk.

He couldn't sleep so he decided to get some work done. When he found that he wasn't able to concentrate, Ari gave up on that, also. He went back into the bedroom and sat near the window, looking out at the magnificent San Francisco skyline.

Ari grabbed his wallet off the small table in the sitting area. He pulled out the photo he carried of April.

"Why can't I move on?" His eyes filled with tears. "I will always love you, April, but the truth is that I've met someone. I never thought I could ever feel love after you died, but I do. I am in love with Natasha. I just wish you could tell me what to do."

He still wasn't sleepy, so he stretched out

on the leather sofa in the sitting room and turned on the TV. His eyelids grew heavy.

Ari was standing in the center of a beautiful park filled with roses of every color imaginable. He turned around slowly, wondering where he was. Suddenly, April appeared in front of him, smiling.

"Am I dead?" he asked.

"No, silly," she responded with a chuckle.

"Where am I?"

Instead of answering him, April asked, "Ari, what is wrong with you?"

"What do you mean?"

"You made me a promise before I had to leave you. Do you remember that promise?"

He nodded. "You wanted me to promise that I could live each day as if it were my last, and that I would hold the memory of our life together in my heart."

She gave him a stern look. "You haven't kept your promise, Ari."

"April, I will not ever get over losing you."

She placed a hand over his heart. "Yes, you will. Our life together is only one chapter in the book of Ari. There is another chapter waiting to be written. Your loving another woman will not change what we shared together. No one can erase those memories."

"How do you know about Natasha?"

"Why do you think I'm here, Ari? You want

*me to release you to love again, but it is you
who won't release me. I am at peace, sweetheart. My time on earth was short but mean-
ingful. I was well-loved and I was able to give
love in return. Releasing me doesn't void what
we shared, Ari."*

"I will always love you, April."

*"I have to go now, but I want you to keep
your promise to me. It is time for chapter two
in the book of Ari."*

Ari woke up with a start.

It was just a dream, but it felt so real to
him. He could still smell the floral scent of
the different species of roses all around
them.

Ari rubbed his arms to ward off the sud-
den chill. This was the first time he'd had a
dream like that about April.

Natasha was in the office typing on her
laptop when Ari came down.

"How long have you been here?" he asked.

"Since seven this morning," she responded. "I had trouble sleeping so I
thought I'd get some work done. What
about you? Why are you down here so
early?"

"I couldn't sleep, either," he confessed.

Natasha glanced over at him but didn't
comment.

Ari finished his coffee then switched to professional mode. "There were some things I noticed in the restaurant on the second floor. I know millions were spent on the main one, but this one needs to be renovated, as well. The furnishings look outdated."

"I agree. It's something you definitely want to consider."

Samuel knocked on the door and said, "Good morning. I am surprised to see the two of you in the office so early."

"We were anxious to get started," Ari said. "I'm actually glad that you're here, Samuel."

Natasha looked as if she was holding her breath, while Samuel looked as if he were going to pass out. Ari bit his lip to keep from laughing out loud.

"I want to discuss renovations for the restaurant on the second floor."

He visibly relaxed.

"Why don't we discuss it in your office," Ari suggested.

He could feel the heat of Natasha's gaze as he followed Samuel out of the room.

Ari didn't see Natasha again until noon.

"Would you like to get out of here for a while?" she asked. "There's this restaurant I'd like to take you to — it's one of my favorite places to eat in San Francisco."

"Sure." He picked up his iPhone and they walked up to the lobby.

"You're going to love this place," she told him.

When they arrived, Ari burst out laughing.

"I knew you would like it."

"A basketball-themed restaurant," he uttered. "Seriously?"

Natasha nodded and pointed to the name. "Burgers and Basketball."

"This is all right," he responded.

They both ordered Kobe Burgers.

Ari's eyes bounced around the restaurant. "This is nice," he said as his gaze landed on the various team jerseys, photos and other basketball memorabilia.

They finished their meal as they talked about the best way to approach his father regarding the renovations for the smaller restaurant in the hotel.

"Why don't I take some pictures," Natasha suggested. "I can also work up a proposal."

"That would be great," he told her.

Natasha insisted on paying for their lunch, so Ari gave in.

On the way back to the hotel, Ari glanced out the window and said, "I don't remember passing this before." He pointed to a bill-board displaying a park filled with exotic roses.

Ari tapped on the privacy window in the limo and said, "Could you please stop at the park on the left?"

"What's going on?" Natasha asked.

"I'll explain later," Ari said. He got out of the car as soon as it came to a halt.

He couldn't believe what he was seeing.

"This is the park that was in my dream," he mumbled to himself. "But how? I've never been here before."

He walked to the center of the park, his eyes surveying the area. *It's the same place,* he thought. *It is the exact same place that I dreamed about.* Even the perfume emitting from the roses was familiar.

Ari looked around, expecting to see April appear at any moment. Although there was no wind, he felt a chill. He heard footsteps and his heart began to race. *She's here.*

"Ari . . ."

He turned around to find Natasha standing there.

"What's going on, Ari?" she asked.

He glanced around once more before saying, "We should get back to the hotel."

Natasha couldn't ignore the sad expression

261

on Ari's face. She had no idea why he wanted to stop at the park, but she suspected it had something to do with April. There was no room in his life for her. He wasn't capable of loving her, and the thought broke her heart. She could no longer work this close to him.

"Why are you so quiet?" Ari asked when they got out of the limo. "Is there something wrong?"

"There's something I need to say to you," Natasha said. "Can you meet me in about an hour in my suite?"

"Sure." He studied her face. "You look upset."

"I'm not, Ari. I am tired, though. I'm done for the day, so I'm just going to stay in my room."

"Do you still want me to come by?"

"Yes."

She walked away before he could see the tears forming in her eyes.

Monica and Joshua were in his bedroom when she entered the suite.

"He's been asking me to take him downstairs to the lake," Monica told her. "He wants to feed the ducks."

Natasha pasted on a smile and said, "That's fine. It might do him some good to get some fresh air."

"I was thinking the same thing. We won't be out there too long." Monica paused a moment. "Would you like to join us?"

"Ari's meeting me here in about forty-five minutes."

She waited until Monica and Joshua left before allowing her tears to fall.

Ari was prompt as always.

Natasha wasted no time in telling him, "When we get back to Los Angeles, I think that you should hire another consultant. I can recommend one from my office or you can go with another firm."

Puzzled, Ari surveyed her face. "I'm not sure I understand, Natasha. Have I done something to offend you?"

"It's nothing like that." Natasha folded her arms across her chest. "The truth is that I can't work with you anymore because of the way I feel about you."

"Natasha, please —"

"Ari, I'm in love with you," Natasha declared, "but it's very clear to me that you still have feelings for —"

This time he interrupted her by saying, "I will always care for April, but Natasha, she's gone, and as much as it pains me, I know that it is time for me to move on."

"That's the problem, Ari. You're not able to move on, but I can't keep waiting around hoping that one day you'll see how much I love you."

"I'm ready to move on . . ." Ari paused a heartbeat before adding, "With you, Natasha."

She opened her mouth to speak, but no words would come.

"I love you," Ari said quietly.

Natasha could hear her heart thumping loudly.

"Hey, did you hear me?"

She nodded.

"I mean it," Ari told her. "I love you and I want you and Joshua in my life."

"When . . . when did you come to this realization?" She was stunned by his declaration. "I saw the pain in your eyes when we were at the park. Ari, I saw the disappointment when you turned around and saw me. It was like you were expecting April. That's when I realized that you didn't have room in your life for me." She shook her head. "Now you're saying that you love me . . ."

"I was expecting April at the park today," he admitted. "But it's because I dreamed that I met her in that very park. Natasha, I've never been in San Francisco and I've never been to that park. I know nothing about it." He took her by the hand and led her over to the sofa.

When they were seated, he continued. "She reminded me of a promise I made to her, and she was upset because I hadn't kept that promise."

Natasha wasn't sure where he was going with this.

"She told me that she was chapter one, but that I needed to start my chapter two . . . with you."

Frowning, she asked, "With me? How could she know anything about me?"

"I know you think I'm crazy, but I'm not. I'm convinced I had this conversation with April. She wants me to move on."

"But what do *you* want, Ari?" Natasha asked.

"It's what I want, also. I think this is why I had the dream in the first place. My heart had been telling me you were my second chance at love, but I was too afraid to open up again. I was afraid to love completely, but you came into my life and now everything has changed."

Natasha stood up and walked over to the fireplace.

He followed her. "What's wrong? I thought you would've been pleased by the news."

"Ari, don't get me wrong. I'm thrilled,

but I can't help but feel as if you're rushing into this. Why don't you take a few days to think about what you really want?"

He turned her around to face him. "You don't think I know my own heart?"

"Ari, I don't mind the memory of her, but I don't want to share you with her ghost." Natasha paused a moment before asking, "Do you understand what I'm saying?"

He nodded.

"Just give yourself a few more days to really sort out your feelings for both of us. I can wait."

"You really are an incredible woman, Natasha."

She smiled. "And don't you ever forget it."

He stepped forward and clasped her body tightly to his. Her body tingled from the contact.

"I love you so much," he whispered.

"I love you, too. I was so afraid that we would never have this chance, but I'm so glad you came to your senses, Ari."

He claimed her lips, his kiss sending spirals of ecstasy through her. Natasha didn't want the moment to end, but she knew that Monica and Joshua would be returning at any moment.

She pulled away from him. "I don't want

Joshua catching us like this. It might confuse him."

"I want to spend more time with him, if you don't mind. I'd like to get to know him better."

"Ari, my son is falling in love with you. His own father rejected him. If . . ." Her voice faltered.

"I am here for the long haul, Natasha. Whatever happens between us won't ever affect my relationship with Joshua. I give you my word."

Joshua was thrilled when he found out they were all going to a musical with Ari. Natasha didn't know who was more excited — her or Joshua. Even Monica seemed to be looking forward to their evening out.

"Hurry up, Mommy," Joshua called from the hallway. "Mr. Ari will be here soon. We don't want to be late."

"We won't be," she promised.

Joshua insisted on answering the door when Ari knocked.

He looked up at him and said, "I'm wearing a suit just like you."

Ari picked him up. "You look quite handsome, Joshua. Your mother is going to have to beat the young ladies off you with a stick."

Joshua blushed.

He glanced over at Natasha and said, "I dressed up for you."

She checked him out from head to toe then smiled in approval.

"The limo's ready," he told them. "We should get going."

They didn't return for four hours.

Ari carried a sleeping Joshua to his bedroom.

He helped Natasha undress the little boy, who stirred only once.

They eased out of the room and sat down in the living room.

Tomorrow they would be leaving early for Seattle, Washington, so Natasha said, "I need to make sure we have everything packed. Thank you for tonight. I haven't seen Joshua this happy in a long time."

"I adore you both."

He kissed her. "I'm going to miss this beautiful face of yours."

"It's only for a few hours."

He gazed at her lovingly. "Good night."

Closing the door behind him, Natasha had a big smile on her face. Ari would make a great father one day. He was patient, caring and seemed to genuinely enjoy his conversations with Joshua. During dinner, they had talked nonstop about car races, video games and math — a subject they both loved.

■ ■ ■ ■

They were going to be in Seattle only for the day because Malcolm wanted Ari back in Los Angeles, so he and Natasha made a list of what they considered to be priorities.

Natasha worked from her suite while he spent most of his day with the hotel management team.

He didn't see Natasha until he knocked on her door at six-thirty that evening.

Joshua selected a movie for them to watch while Ari ordered dinner for them. Monica had planned to retreat to her room, but they refused to let her.

"C'mon," Ari told her. "We can all watch a movie together. Let's have some fun before we head back to California tomorrow morning."

"Okay, if you insist," she said finally.

"We insist, don't we, Mr. Ari?"

"We sure do."

"*The Incredibles* is my favorest movie," Joshua announced.

"Favorite," Natasha and Monica said in unison.

Ari laughed. It had been a long time since he felt this content. He was with a woman he loved and a little boy he desperately wanted as a part of his family. He hadn't realized just how much he wanted to be a father until now.

They enjoyed dinner together and afterward watched *The Incredibles.* This was Ari's first time ever seeing the movie.

Monica retreated to her room as soon as the movie ended, while Joshua pleaded to see another one. When Natasha refused to give in, he tried another tactic. "Can I please watch a little bit of *Chicken Run?*"

"Just a little bit," she repeated.

Pleased, Joshua climbed in Ari's lap. Natasha sat beside him.

Fifteen minutes later, they were all fast asleep.

Ari woke up and eased off the couch. He laid Joshua down beside his mother. He watched them a moment before grabbing one of the cushions off another chair and laying down on the floor. He considered going to his own suite, but he didn't want to leave Natasha and Joshua.

CHAPTER 19

The weekend after their trip, Ari took Natasha and Joshua to Pacific Palisades. They were going out there to discuss the upcoming barbecue.

As soon as they arrived, Barbara called them into the living room. "Is there something you two wish to tell us?" she asked.

Malcolm walked up to his wife and placed an arm around her. "Sugar, I think we already know what's going on."

Ari took Natasha's hand. "We're in love."

"Me, too," Joshua said, taking Ari's other hand.

They all laughed.

Sage strolled into the room. "Well, it's certainly about time you two got together."

"Or not," another young woman uttered.

Natasha glanced over at Ari, who said, "I didn't know you were in town, Zaire."

"Honey, don't be rude to our guests," Barbara said.

She walked up to Natasha, her gaze direct.

Joshua walked over to where his mother was standing. "My name is Joshua. Who are you?"

"This is my baby sister," Ari stated. "Her name is Zaire."

"Zaa-ere," Joshua repeated. "I've never heard that name before. I kinda like it."

Fascinated, Zaire watched Joshua for a moment and then looked back at Natasha. "He's your son?"

Natasha responded, "Yes, he is."

"Do you think . . ." She paused. "Can he have some ice cream?"

Ari put an arm around his sister. Zaire was outspoken and quick-tempered, but when it came to a child, she was putty. She was trying to compose herself in front of Joshua.

He took her by the hand. "I like your name, Zaa-ere, but I want to call you something else. Can I call you Zaa?"

She nodded. "You are absolutely adorable."

"Is that why you're about to cry?"

"Yes," she managed.

"I like you, Zaa. Can we be friends?"

Zaire glanced over at Natasha and smiled. "It's very nice to meet you."

"You, too, Zaire."

"Joshua and I will be in the kitchen eating ice cream. After that, where we are will depend on what he wants to do."

Ari and Natasha laughed.

Zaire took Joshua to the kitchen.

"She didn't know about Joshua?" Natasha asked Ari.

"No, I didn't say anything."

"She has never let anyone of us call her by a nickname, ever," Sage said in disbelief. "Wow. Joshua has her wrapped around his fingers."

Malcolm and Barbara agreed.

There were only two members of the Alexander family missing: Drayden and Kellen. Everyone else was present at the house.

They spotted Franklin in the backyard talking to the landscaper. "Ari, I'll be back," Natasha told him. "I want to speak to Franklin."

She left the room.

"She's charming," Barbara said. "I can tell she makes you happy, Ari."

"Mom, I love her with my heart and soul." He walked over to the window. "I never thought I'd say that about anyone other than April, but it's true."

"Franklin, how are you?" Natasha asked.

He smiled. "I'm fine. From the looks of

things, you and Ari are getting along quite well."

"We are," she confirmed with a grin.

"I am happy for you both," he said.

"How are things between you and Tammie?"

"She is still very angry with me, and I can't say I blame her. I walked out on her and my wife."

"Why haven't you told them what happened to you?"

He held his head down. "Because I am ashamed."

Natasha touched his arm. "You are a good man, Franklin. Tell your daughter the truth. Tell your wife. She never divorced you — maybe there's a reason why."

"You are a hopeless romantic."

Natasha laughed.

"How is Joshua?" Franklin asked.

"He's doing great," she responded. "In fact, you will probably see him at some point. He's in the kitchen eating ice cream with Zaire."

Franklin raised his eyebrows in surprise. "Really?"

"Yes, she has a heart for children, and when she saw Joshua she was overcome with so much emotion. But then she just took him under her wing."

"She is fiercely protective of her family."

"I can tell. She wasn't exactly thrilled to hear that Ari and I were involved until she met Joshua. I'm not real sure how she feels about me, but she is wonderful to my son. That's all I care about."

"It has been nice talking to you," Franklin said. "I don't want to keep you away from the family."

Natasha gave him a hug.

Ari was standing on the patio when she turned around. He waved and smiled.

She waved back.

"Franklin is a good man," he said when Natasha reached him. "I'm glad he's a part of our family now."

"This is the one fundamental difference between Robert and your family. You all treat employees as if they are members of your family. Robert was a good man, but employees were just that — employees."

"This is who we are, Natasha. We believe that if we respect and treat our employees like family and they are happy and secure, they will be more productive."

She agreed. "I love that you care about people."

He wrapped an arm around her. "In the mood for a swim?"

"You just want to see me in a bikini."

Ari grinned. "You brought a bikini to change into?"

Natasha shook her head. "Sorry to disappoint you, sweetie."

He covered her mouth with his own.

They heard giggling and stepped away from one another.

"Zaa, did you see that?" Joshua asked. "Mr. Ari was kissing my mommy."

"Yeah, I saw it."

Natasha looked at Zaire, who smiled and said, "You make him happy. Ari deserves that."

"He makes me happy, as well."

"Joshua and I are going to change into swimsuits. Oh, you don't have to worry. I am a certified lifeguard. We are just going to hang out in the shallow end."

"Thank you for spending time with my baby."

She glanced down at Joshua and said, "He's adorable."

Blaze walked out on the patio. "So are we going to get in the pool or what?"

Ari was truly happy. He hadn't felt this alive in a long time, and it was because of the beautiful woman beside him, and her son.

Robert DePaul had been dead for three

months to the day. This was also the day that the Alexander family hosted a barbecue to celebrate their arrival in Los Angeles. Natasha arrived, dressed in a silk sundress and heels.

She halted her steps when Ari came out of the house dressed in a pair of jeans and a polo shirt.

"Is that what you're wearing?" she asked.

"Yeah," he responded. "It's a barbecue."

"I know, but I thought . . ." Natasha shook her head. "I didn't think you would be dressed so casually."

"Where we're from, we don't dress up for a barbecue."

Natasha chewed on her bottom lip. There was going to be media coverage, the VIP guests . . .

"Don't worry, sweetheart," Ari whispered in her ear. "Everyone will have a good time."

Natasha was worried, however.

His mother had on a denim skirt while Sage had on a cute halter dress and sandals.

"Wow, you look great, Natasha," Sage said. "You do know that this is a barbecue, don't you?"

She smiled. "I know. I just thought it was more of a dressy event."

"Do you want to change into a pair of shorts or something?"

"I have a pair of silver sandals in the car," Natasha told her. "I'll just slip them on."

The guests arrived dressed similarly to Natasha.

"Don't these people know how to dress for a barbecue?" Barbara asked her husband.

"I guess not," he responded.

Malcolm welcomed everyone, and then said, "We want you all to have a good time. Take off your fancy shoes and kick back and relax. We're simple people, but we like to have a good time."

On the menu were hamburgers, veggie burgers, barbecue chicken, shrimp and ribs. For sides, guests could choose potato salad, cucumber salad, baked beans, corn on the cob, macaroni salad and coleslaw.

"The food is delicious and everyone seems to be having a great time, including the reporters covering the event," Natasha whispered. She and Ari walked around, pausing here and there to talk to some of the guests.

Ari's eyes traveled the yard. "Everybody looks happy."

"I have to admit that you were right again, Ari. Having everyone see you and your family like this — it's good publicity."

When the party ended, Natasha announced, "I want you to know that you are all the sweethearts of the hospitality industry. Your sincerity and Southern charm worked in your favor. I actually overheard one reporter refer to you as a more sophisticated version of the Beverly Hillbillies." When she saw the expressions on their faces, she quickly added, "But I don't think he meant it as insulting."

After a moment, they all burst into laughter.

Natasha glanced over at Ari, who explained, "It was one of our favorite TV shows."

She sighed in relief. "Oh, I thought maybe you were offended."

"We don't offend that easily," Malcolm told her.

They settled down in empty chairs around the patio.

"I love being around your family," Natasha said. "I admire your strength as a family."

Ari finished off his water. "A family is at its strongest when they stick together. Our parents taught us to be individuals, but as a family, we function as a unit."

Natasha couldn't take her eyes off him.

"What is it?" Ari asked. "Do I have food on my face or something?"

"No," she responded. "I was just thinking about how much I love you. Sometimes, I feel like I'm dreaming. I can't believe that I have such a wonderful man in my life."

He kissed her. "It's not a dream, sweetheart. We are together, and there isn't a thing in the world that can tear us apart."

An image of Harold DePaul entered Natasha's mind, sending a wave of apprehension through her.

CHAPTER 20

"Harold, what are you doing here?" Natasha demanded. She didn't bother to hide the irritation in her voice. "I would appreciate it if you would call first before just showing up at my door."

"Why? Are you expecting someone?"

"That's none of your business," she snapped. "Now, what do you want, Harold?"

"Oh, but I'm afraid it is," he said as he held out a large manila envelope to her. "Perhaps you'd better take a look at these."

Natasha couldn't hide her surprised reaction. Harold had photographs of her and Ari in San Francisco, in Seattle, at the barbecue and other times, including their date last night. "Where did you get this?" she demanded. "Do you have someone watching me?"

"I'm merely protecting my interests."

"You have no right to invade my privacy like this." Natasha glowered at him and turned away. "I can't believe you would do something like this to me."

"Natasha, I wanted to make sure I was right in trusting you," Harold told her.

She threw the pictures down on the coffee table. "You are the one who can't be trusted."

"Oh, really? Tell me something, Natasha. How long have you been sleeping with the enemy?"

She slapped him as hard as she could. "Get out of my house *now.*"

"Or what?" Harold questioned. "You are really in no position to make threats against me. If you don't want lover boy to know whose camp you are really in, you'd better make sure the DePaul Group goes public. I have everything in place. We are just waiting to hear from you."

"I didn't understand until now why your uncle didn't leave everything to you. It's because he knew what you were about."

Harold dismissed her words with a slight wave of his hand. "My uncle has always been an emotional fool."

"You'd better hope that none of your skeletons start coming out of the closet," Natasha warned.

He laughed. "I'm so much smarter than

that, Natasha. You of all people should know this."

"Get out of my house." Natasha was careful to keep her voice down. "I don't know what happened to you, Harold. You disgust me."

"You're much too good for Ari."

"He's a better man than you are, Harold," she shot back.

He glared at her for a moment before slamming the door shut.

The nurse came rushing out of Joshua's room. "Is everything okay?"

"Yes, everything's fine," she lied. "Harold DePaul was just here and he slammed the door on the way out by accident."

Monica accepted her response without question. She turned and went back upstairs.

Natasha rubbed her arms up and down. She didn't need Harold as an enemy. A negative word from him could ruin her business. Although she didn't want to work with Harold any longer, she didn't want to anger him, either.

Ari had just arrived when Harold walked out of Natasha's building. "What is he doing here?" he whispered.

He stayed in his car, watching Harold. The

283

man looked furious over something, leading Ari to wonder if something just happened between him and Natasha. *What is going on?*

Ari got out of his car just as Harold drove away.

He took the elevator to her floor and got out. He stood outside her door, silently debating whether or not to question her about Harold.

Natasha opened the door and was surprised to see him. "Hey, you . . . I didn't expect to see you today."

"Obviously," he responded.

Natasha's smile disappeared and she quickly surveyed his face. "Honey, are you okay?"

She stepped back to let him enter the condo.

"So what have you been doing all day?"

"Nothing much," she responded. "Monica is here with Joshua, so I was about to run some errands. Are you interested in riding along with me?"

"Why don't I drive," Ari suggested. "It'll help me with learning the city."

He couldn't decide whether or not to bring up Harold's name. Although she was trying hard to hide it, Ari could tell that Natasha was upset.

"You don't look like yourself," he told her. "Do you need to talk about anything?"

Natasha shook her head no.

"There's nothing you need to tell me?"

She glanced over at him. "Why would you ask me that?"

"You just look like you're upset about something. I thought maybe you needed to talk."

It was apparent that Natasha wasn't going to open up, which left Ari suspicious. He couldn't help but wonder if something was going on between her and Harold.

Until he found the truth, he would not be able to trust Natasha with his whole heart.

Harold called her, but she let the call go to voice mail.

Natasha wanted to tell Ari everything, but she feared losing him. The way Ari was acting earlier still weighed heavily on her mind.

He suspects something.

I have to be honest with Ari, she decided. *I can't hurt the man I love or his family, but I need him to understand that I couldn't risk losing my son to leukemia, either.*

She walked down to his office, but Ari wasn't there. When she checked with his assistant, Natasha was told that he was out of the office but was expected back at any moment.

Natasha checked her watch. She had a staff meeting and needed to get back to her own office. "Tell Ari that I need to speak with him. I have an appointment right now, but I'll be back in a couple of hours."

Harold called her cell phone once more. She ignored that call, as well. She was not in the mood for another argument.

Ari was returning just as she drove out of the parking lot.

Natasha tried to get his attention, but he wasn't looking in her direction. She decided that she was going to have a conversation with him as soon as she returned. It was time for her to tell Ari everything. If she expected to have any type of future with him, she had to be honest.

CHAPTER 21

"Dad, I'm telling you that there is something going on between Natasha and Harold. I saw the man leave her building with my own eyes." He was sitting in Malcolm's office discussing what had transpired the day before.

"They attended college together, and didn't she mention that they were friends?"

"Yeah, but just how close are they?" Ari wondered aloud.

Malcolm settled back in his chair. "Have you asked Natasha about this?"

"No, I wanted to talk to you first," Ari stated. "I'm pretty sure that Harold was behind the company wanting to buy the hotel chain. So I can't help but wonder what else they are plotting."

His thoughts were disquieting. It had occurred to him that maybe Natasha's interest in him wasn't real. Ari felt his heart ache at the thought that she was using him.

He called his assistant and said, "Could you please ask Natasha to come to my office?"

"You wanted to see me?" Natasha asked, walking into his office.

"Please come in and shut the door behind you," Ari said.

Natasha did as she was told. "Is there something wrong?" she asked, sitting down in one of the chairs facing his desk.

"I need to know something," Ari said.

"Okay," she responded.

He decided the direct approach was best. "Natasha, what's going on between you and Harold DePaul?"

"Are you serious? Ari, it's nothing like what you're thinking."

Ari responded, "I've never been more serious. I need to know if there is something between you and Harold."

"No," she uttered. "Harold and I went to college together and I thought he was a friend, but this is the extent of our relationship."

"No, I'm sure there's more to that relationship than just attending the same college with the man. Natasha, I am not a fool, so don't treat me like one. Harold and his family are the ones wanting to buy the hotel chain, right?"

The animation left her eyes as she realized where this conversation was going. She nodded.

Ari settled back in his chair. "Tell me something, Natasha. Where do your loyalties lie?"

"I am on your side, Ari," she responded a little too quickly. "I am on your father's side."

Her telephone rang, interrupting their conversation.

"I'm sorry, but I need to take this call," she announced. "It's the hospital."

"Hello, this is Natasha."

Her facial expression changed to one of shock. "I'm sure there must be some type of misunderstanding," Ari heard Natasha tell the doctor. "I need to make a couple of phone calls and I'll get back to you."

When she hung up, Natasha asked, "Can we finish this conversation later? I really need to take care of something."

She was clearly upset.

"Sure," Ari said. "We can talk tonight."

"Thank you." Natasha turned around and walked briskly to the door. "I have to go out for a while."

Ari waited until she stepped into the elevator. He caught the next one and headed down to the lobby.

Harold had placed a stop payment on the last check he sent to her, which caused her payment to the hospital to be returned.

As soon as she walked out of the building, Natasha placed a call to Harold. "Do you want to tell me exactly what is going on?" she demanded. "You are playing with my son's life, and I don't like it." Her voice broke miserably.

"I warned you, Natasha," he responded tersely. "It's pretty clear to me that you've chosen Malcolm Alexander and his brood over the DePaul family, so why don't you get them to foot your son's doctor bills?"

"Harold, how could you be so cruel? This is an innocent child. I did everything you told me to do. I held up my end of the bargain."

"They still have the properties, Natasha. They are not going to sell off shares — how can I get my hotels back, Natasha?"

"I can't make them sell if they don't want to, Harold. I told you from the beginning that there were no guarantees."

"And I told you that I wanted results. Why should I pay you when I'm not getting a return on my investment? Although I'm sure that we can come to some sort of agreement. I can take care of you and Joshua if you'd —"

Natasha hung up on him.

As she wiped away her tears, Natasha's mind was busy at work, trying to figure out her next move. She turned around to find Ari standing there.

The expression on his face told Natasha what she feared had come true. It was obvious that he had heard her conversation with Harold DePaul. Added to her disappointment was a feeling of guilt.

"Please let me explain," she began.

Ari held up his hand to silence her. "I guess everything we suspected about you is true. We did have a traitor among us."

"It's not what you think."

He shook his head regretfully. "I beg to differ. I have no tolerance when someone is out to hurt my family." Ari's expression hardened. "I don't like being used, either."

"Please, just listen to what I have to say before you judge me, Ari," Natasha pleaded. "Please."

"I've heard enough. Oh, your services are no longer needed. You're fired."

"Ari . . ."

He didn't respond and just kept walking.

Natasha considered going after him but

decided that he needed some time to calm down. She prayed Ari would find it in his heart to forgive her.

Ari wasn't surprised when he didn't hear from Natasha. *I knew she couldn't be trusted, so why did I let her into my heart?* The question reverberated over and over in his head. *I should've seen this coming,* he thought. *I knew Harold was up to something, but I had no idea he would take it this far.*

The doorbell sounded, cutting into his thoughts.

Ari went to answer the door. He was surprised to see Sage standing there. "What are you doing here?" Ari asked. "I thought you were supposed to be in Santa Barbara today."

"I'm going up later this afternoon," she responded, walking inside the residence. "I wanted to make sure you were okay."

Ari closed the door behind her. "I guess you talked to Natasha."

She nodded her head. "She called me and told me everything."

"Don't you feel just a little bit betrayed?" he asked her.

Sage met his gaze. "Yeah, I do. I told Natasha exactly what I thought of her and Harold. I really let her have it for the way she hurt you."

"I haven't said anything to Dad yet."

"What are you going to tell him?"

Ari shrugged. "I don't know. The truth, I guess."

"I don't think you want to say anything to Zaire. You know she wasn't too thrilled to hear that you were involved with Natasha. She never trusted her from the beginning."

"Turns out she was right," he mumbled to himself.

Sage placed a hand on his arm. "Ari, I'm angry with Natasha, but everything she did was for Joshua."

"She could have come to us at any point and confessed what was going on, but she didn't. Natasha continued the charade. Had she just come to me with the truth, we could have worked through it."

"I agree with you, Ari, but I also see Natasha's side of it. She was scared."

"I don't trust her, Sage. If I can't trust her, then we can't be in a relationship. What Natasha and I had is over." Ari shook his head. "I'm not sure it ever really began."

Ari continued to deal with his broken heart by working long hours. By the time he made it home, he was too exhausted to think about anything other than going to bed.

After his shower, Ari checked his iPhone to see if he had missed any calls. He opened his email and saw one from Joshua.

Mr. Ari

I am riting you to say I am sory for makin you mad. I don't no wat I did but I am very very sory. I hope we can still be frinds. I miss you.

Joshua

Ari wrote him back, explaining that he had been very busy with work and that is why he had not been by for a visit. He assured him that he was not mad and that Joshua would be hearing from him soon. He wrote in his email that Joshua could email him any time.

Despite what was going on between him and Natasha, Joshua could not get caught up in the middle. He would have to sit down with Natasha to see if there was a way he could remain in Joshua's life.

Ari considered calling Natasha, but he really wasn't ready to talk to her. He was still very angry and disappointed.

He didn't sleep well that night. Ari tossed and turned, his mind plagued with dreams of Joshua calling out for him and of Natasha pleading with him to forgive her. He loved her and without her in his life, Ari felt as if there was huge hole where his heart used to be. He felt her absence as deeply as he had felt April's death.

Ari got up before his alarm clock sounded. He made breakfast, although he didn't feel much like eating.

Blaze walked out of the bedroom. "Something smells delicious."

"There's more than enough food," Ari said.

"I just spoke to Dad. He wants you and I to attend the meeting with Ira this morning."

Ari nodded. "That's fine."

"How are you?" Blaze asked as he poured himself a cup of coffee.

"I'm okay," Ari responded. A pain squeezed his heart as he thought of Natasha.

"I'm sorry."

Ari looked over at his brother. "For what?"

"I pushed you to get with Natasha. I had no idea she was working with Harold."

He shrugged in nonchalance. "It doesn't matter anymore."

"You're in love with her," Blaze stated.

"I'll get over it." Ari finished off his juice and then said, "I'm going to the gym for about an hour."

Blaze nodded as he spooned scrambled eggs onto his plate. "Thanks for breakfast, man."

"Enjoy," Ari uttered as he made his way to the door.

He returned home an hour later to shower and dress for work.

Malcolm, Ari and Blaze met with Ira Goodman at his law firm. They were there to discuss the situation with the Nevada hotels.

"The applications for the permits are pending," Malcolm announced. "I offered fifty thousand dollars to get this thing settled. Harold really left a mess behind."

"I think it's time we had a meeting with this man," Blaze said. "We've kept this quiet to protect our grandfather's name, but we don't have to protect Harold. This was all his doing."

Ari agreed.

"Not just yet," Malcolm interjected. "Let's get this settled once and for all. Then we will meet with Harold DePaul."

CHAPTER 22

"Mommy, did I do something bad?"

Natasha shook her head. "No, baby. Why do you think that you did?"

"I think Mr. Ari is mad with me."

She felt an instant's squeezing hurt. Natasha picked up her son, holding him close to her. "He's not mad with you, Joshua. He's been very busy at work. That's all."

"Are you sure?"

"I am. He will come by to see you soon." Natasha was not going to let Joshua be affected by her actions. She knew that Ari cared deeply for him.

"I sent him an email, but I don't know if he emailed me back."

Joshua hadn't been feeling well over the past couple of days, so he hadn't been working on the computer.

"Would you like for me to check for you?"

Joshua nodded. "I hope he wrote me back."

I do, too, Natasha thought. She knew that Ari would never take his anger out on Joshua.

"You have an email from Ari," she announced.

"Mommy, can you read it to me?"

"I sure can." Ari's words touched her heart, bringing tears to her eyes. "He promises to see you very soon."

She stayed with Joshua until he fell asleep.

Natasha left the room quietly and walked across the hall to her bedroom.

She picked up the telephone and dialed. "Ari, it's me, Natasha."

"I recognized the number," he said.

"I won't keep you," she quickly interjected. "I wanted to thank you for emailing Joshua. He's been worried that you were angry with him. I know that we are at odds right now, but I'm hoping you will continue to have a relationship with Joshua."

"I'd like that, Natasha. I know that I can't see him right now, but maybe in a couple of weeks or so."

"Ari, I'm not sure Joshua can wait that long. You are welcome to see him anytime. I can arrange to be somewhere else."

"I'm not going to run you away from your home," he told her. "We are both adults. I'm sure we can be cordial to one another."

"I just didn't want you avoiding my son because you're angry with me. He looks up to you, Ari, and you have been the closest thing to a father he's ever had."

"How about I come by sometime this weekend?" he offered. "Will that be okay with you?"

"That would be great. He will be so excited." She paused a moment, then added, "Thank you, Ari."

"Tell Joshua I will see him on Saturday."

Natasha hung up the phone, tears rolling down her cheeks. She had lost the one man who ever truly loved her.

Hearing Natasha's voice on the other end of the line only increased his heartache.

He wanted to hate her, but he couldn't.

His heart wouldn't let him.

William DePaul knocked on his door.

Masking his hurt, Ari gestured for him to enter.

"I thought you might want to see this," William said as he handed Ari a press release. "And for what it's worth, Natasha was just as much a victim. My brother only cares about himself. Uncle Robert knew about some of the underhanded things Harold was doing, but before he could do anything about it, he became ill."

"Did you make your uncle aware of what was going on?" Ari asked.

"I did," William acknowledged. "But Harold kept me in the dark, as well."

"I am glad to have you on board, William."

He smiled. "I am grateful for the opportunity to meet other members of my family. Your father is an extraordinary man and I'm glad we're getting to know one another." William turned and headed to the door. "I need to get back to my office. I'm meeting with a new vendor."

"Thanks, William," Ari said. He read the press release in his hand.

Blythewood Appoints Harold DePaul Director of Operations

Blythewood Hotels & Resorts, the premier manager of ultra-luxury properties throughout the world, is thrilled to announce the appointment of Harold DePaul as Director of Operations of The Rosen Hotel Hollywood, which is scheduled to open early next year. The hotel, currently undergoing a full restoration, originally opened in 1901 and was and will be again Hollywood's most elegant and historic hotel. Mr. DePaul will oversee all areas of the hotel, which is being developed by Blythewood Development Ltd., which is part of the Wilmington Group.

With a decade of experience and success in the management of luxury hotel operations, DePaul joins Blythewood Hotels & Resorts following his most recent position as Managing Director of the DePaul Hotel Group. DePaul will manage Blythewood's newest addition and second California property to its already outstanding collection of notable properties.

"Blythewood is committed to creating world-renowned hotels and resorts, and we are pleased to have the protégé of Robert DePaul open this spectacular property," said David Hanson, Chief Operating Officer of Blythewood Hotels & Resorts. "His years of experience and wealth of knowledge in the hospitality industry are well suited to lead efforts at the Rosen Hotel Hollywood."

"Maybe this will keep Harold busy and away from my father," Ari uttered. "One thing for sure. It's definitely time for a face-to-face."

He pushed away from his desk and walked down to Malcolm's office. "Dad, I know how to get Harold DePaul to stay away from us permanently."

Malcolm removed his glasses and settled back in his chair. "I'm listening."

Malcolm had his secretary contact Harold and demand a meeting within the hour. While they waited, Ari and his father went over what they planned to say to Harold. Blaze joined them a few minutes later.

The telephone rang.

"He's here," Malcolm announced when he hung up.

"What is this all about?" Harold questioned. "Have you finally come to your senses and decided to walk away from the hotel properties?"

"Why would we do that?" Malcolm asked. He sat in his chair, arms folded across his chest.

"Then why did you summon me over here?" Harold glanced over at Ari and asked, "How is Natasha?"

Ari didn't respond, although deep down he wanted to rip the man to shreds.

Malcolm removed his eyeglasses and set them on the desk. "I don't know if you're aware that this company is under investigation, or should I say, was under investigation."

"What have you done?"

"The appropriate question is what have *you* done?" Ari interjected. "The Nevada State Contractors Board was investigating a report that remodeling had taken place at the two properties there, without permits."

Harold's eyes registered his surprise. He struggled to regain his composure. "Where did they get that ridiculous information?"

"From a former employee of the construction company you used," Malcolm stated. "Apparently, he phoned four local regulatory groups back in April."

"Obviously, there's been some mistake," Harold said. "We have permits for everything we've done."

"Those permits were forged, Harold," Ari stated, "by you. We had the handwriting analyzed. An employee with Licenses and Permits confessed that he was paid a large sum of money to file the forgeries, but he never filed the falsified documents for fear it would all lead back to him."

"Which it did anyway," Malcolm said.

Harold no longer looked as confident as he did when he first arrived.

"Fred Bancroft had a lot to tell us about you and your secret deals," Malcolm told him. "He didn't just phone those four offices — he also made sure that your uncle knew what you had done. He told Franklin everything."

Ari gave Harold a hard stare as he said, "We have a firm paper trail all leading back to you. And this is just one avenue of deceit. We have other trails leading to greed, cheap materials, misappropriated funds . . ."

"So what is it that you want from me?" Harold interjected.

"I want you to stay away from me and my family," Malcolm stated. "You set all of this in motion with your deceit. Your uncle knew all about the personal expenses you billed to the hotel. He knew everything, but what he hated most was the way you treated the employees."

"You're not a very popular man around here," Ari said.

"I don't care what a bunch of wage earners think of me," he huffed.

"You may want to change that attitude because pretty soon, everyone, including your new employer, will hear about the things you've done," Blaze advised.

"This can't be happening to me," Harold muttered.

Malcolm rose to his feet and walked from around the desk. "Oh, but it is, cousin. How do you think your new employer will feel about you if news of what you did to your own uncle comes to light?"

Harold's head popped up. "This doesn't have to become public knowledge."

"No, it doesn't, as long as you stay away from my family," Malcolm responded.

"And Natasha," Ari interjected.

"The information will stay buried as long as you honor our wishes," Malcolm said. "I've settled with the Nevada State Contractors Board. All fines have been paid, and we have legitimate permits in place. However, *you* are going to reimburse this company for every penny we spent to fix this mess."

Harold pulled out his checkbook, but Malcolm stated, "Certified check only."

"How do I know that you'll keep your word?" Harold demanded.

"We haven't said anything thus far," Ari responded. "We've had this information for weeks. Oh, there is one more thing. I want you to give Natasha the money you promised her. She did exactly what you asked of her."

"Apparently, not well enough," Harold grumbled. "I'll have the certified checks delivered via messenger later today."

Malcolm handed him a piece of paper. "This is what you owe the company. It's really only a fraction, but we will accept this payment as a settlement. Have a good day, cousin."

Defeated, Harold sighed in resignation, then uttered, "You, too, cousin."

CHAPTER 23

Natasha was surprised to find Sage Alexander standing at her door. This was about the last person she expected to see. "I didn't think you were ever going to talk to me again." She stepped aside to let the woman enter her condo.

"You did it for your son," Sage said, removing her purse off her shoulder. "I'm not a mother, but I understand it. It was wrong, though, but I know that you're not a bad person. Besides, you're my only real friend out here, so I forgive you."

"Thank you for saying that, Sage."

The two women embraced.

"I was just about to have a salad for lunch," Natasha announced. "Would you care to join me? There's more than enough."

"Sure," Sage responded. "Do you mind if I freshen up? I spent the morning going through a mountain of paperwork."

Natasha pointed in the direction of the

guest bathroom.

"He's as miserable as you are," Sage stated when she returned.

Natasha fought back tears. "I really love him."

"Ari loves you, too," Sage assured her. "He's just feeling a little betrayed right now."

She nodded in understanding. "I guess I'd feel the same way if I were in his shoes."

"He's going to come around — just give him some time."

Natasha shook her head. "Ari may have feelings for me, but I really don't think he's going to ever trust me again."

They sat down to the table.

"Did you see the article in the newspaper about Harold DePaul?" Sage asked. "William gave my father and Ari copies of the actual press release that went out."

Natasha nodded. "I hope this means he won't be bothering your family anymore."

Sage wiped her mouth on the end of the napkin. "I don't think he will. He had a meeting with my father and Ari earlier today."

"Really? About what?"

"I overheard my dad saying that Harold had done some stuff behind Robert's back and it's come back to bite him in the butt."

"I'm not surprised," Natasha stated. "But I hope your father won't fall for Harold's lies. He will act like he's going along with everything, but he's not going to give up this easily."

"Well, whatever he's planning, he's messing with the wrong family." Sage stuck a forkful of salad into her mouth.

"Ari, she did it for her son," Blaze was saying. "Can you say you wouldn't have done the same thing?"

"Natasha had plenty of chances to tell me what was going on. I would've done anything for Joshua. She should've trusted me."

"Well, she trusted you with her heart, Ari," Blaze pointed out.

"I trusted her with mine, too."

"Are you telling me that you two can't get past this?" Blaze finished off his drink. "Man, you love the woman. Are you just going to walk away like this?"

"I can't believe you're being so forgiving," Ari said. "This is so out of character for you."

"She's a good person."

Ari didn't respond.

"I've met enough women with tricks up their sleeves that I can see them a mile away," Blaze stated. "Natasha's not like those women. Harold DePaul took advantage of her, plain and simple."

"That may be the case, but Natasha should have come to me with the truth."

"I agree with you, Ari, but have you truly considered the position she was in? Why wouldn't she align herself with Harold DePaul? They were friends in college. She didn't know you or much about our family. She was loyal to Robert and the DePaul family."

"I understand all that," Ari said. "But once she decided to work for our father, she should've told Harold what he could do with his money."

"Yet you forced Harold to give her the money he promised her."

Ari shrugged in nonchalance. "She certainly earned it."

"You did it because you still love her," Blaze countered.

"Yeah, I still love Natasha," Ari admitted, "but how can I ever trust her again?"

"Natasha needs you, Ari," Sage told him when he answered his cell phone. "Something is wrong with Joshua. They are at Cedar-Sinai Medical Center. He's been sick for the past few days, but now it's gotten worse."

Ari immediately went into action mode. He picked up his keys and was heading to the door. "Thanks for letting me know, Sage. I'll call you later. I need to get to Natasha."

Ari prayed the entire drive over, pleading with God to spare the little boy's life. He had come to love Joshua as much as he would his own child and couldn't bear the thought of losing him.

He had planned on visiting Joshua on Saturday, but now he regretted not having gone sooner. He never should have let his anger at Natasha keep him from the little boy.

Natasha was clearly surprised to see him walking toward her in the sterile corridor on the third floor. "Ari, what are you doing here?"

"I came to be here for you and Joshua. Sage called and told me what happened. She wanted me to tell you that she will come to the hospital as soon as she can."

A tear slid down Natasha's cheek. "I'm really scared."

Ari wrapped his arms around her. "Honey, it's going to be okay," he whispered, holding her close. "Joshua is going to pull through. He's a tough little boy."

She shook her head. "We don't know that.

He's so weak, and his fever wouldn't go down."

"We have to believe that Joshua is going to be fine. We have to hold on to our faith."

Natasha wiped away her tears. "I'm trying to be strong, but this is my baby. He's all I have, Ari, and I can't lose him." In that moment, Ari fully understood why she had agreed to help Harold.

"You won't," Ari responded. "How long has he been sick?"

"About three or four days, but his temperature was at 101 today," Natasha replied.

"Why didn't you tell me?"

"I didn't want you coming over just because Joshua was sick. I wanted you to come because you wanted to see him."

The doctor arrived to talk to Natasha. She insisted that Ari stay by her side.

"We are going to keep Joshua in the pediatric ICU until we can get the fever down and the infection under control."

"Please, do whatever you have to do to save my son," she pleaded. "Don't let Joshua die."

Ari led her over to a nearby chair. He sat down beside her.

Natasha wiped her face with the damp tissue she had been holding. "Thank you for coming, Ari."

"I wouldn't be any other place, Natasha. I hope you know that."

"Things are so tense between us," she began. "I —"

Ari cut her off by saying, "We need to focus on your son right now — making sure Joshua has everything he needs is what's most important right now."

"He's why I agreed to help Harold in the first place," Natasha blurted. "I wanted the medical treatments for Joshua, and working with him was the only way I could afford them."

Ari nodded in understanding. He pulled an envelope out of his jacket pocket. "Harold had this delivered to us yesterday."

"What is it?"

"It's a check for the money he owes you."

Natasha shook her head no. "I don't want his money. I've put the building Robert gave me up for sale and I'm closing my business."

"There are no other strings attached."

"I don't care," Natasha uttered. "Harold DePaul can keep his money." She snatched the envelope and tore it up. "I never should have gotten involved with him in the first place. I don't know what I was thinking."

Natasha glanced up at him. "How did you get him to do this?"

"Shortly before Robert died, he was informed by a former employee that the renovations for the Nevada hotels were done without a valid permit. He also called several agencies. The Nevada State Contractors Board launched an investigation."

"I never heard about any of this," she responded.

"My father urged them to keep news of the investigation quiet."

"Is that why you wanted to see the permits and licenses the first day you started?"

Ari nodded.

"Why didn't you say anything to me?" Natasha asked.

"Because I wasn't sure I could trust you," he responded quietly.

"I see." She folded her arms across her chest. "I guess you should've trusted your instincts about me."

"Natasha, I want you to know that you will never have to worry about Joshua's medical care. I am going to make sure he has every advantage. You don't have to close your business or sell your building."

"You are such a wonderful man, Ari. I love that you care so much about Joshua, but what I did to your family wasn't right. I wish I could say that I regret my actions, but the truth is that I don't. It was for my child. As much as I appreciate your wanting to help, Ari, I have to say no. I won't take advantage of your kindness. I can't do this to you. *Not anymore.*"

"Natasha, this isn't about you, sweetheart. I'm doing this for Joshua."

She opened her mouth to speak, but Ari held up his hand to stop her. "This is not negotiable."

Natasha dropped her shoulders in resignation.

"When was the last time you had something to eat?" Ari inquired.

"I don't remember," she responded. "Maybe at dinner last night. I had some tea this morning."

"Sweetheart, you need to eat something."

"I'm not hungry."

"Natasha, I'm going to the cafeteria to get you some soup. You really need to put something in your stomach. Joshua doesn't need his mother passing out."

"Ari, thank you."

He pulled her into his arms. "We will get through this together."

"I'm so glad you're here with me." She started to cry.

He held her in his arms until she stopped crying.

Natasha stood up and walked into a

nearby ladies' room to wash her face. She returned a few minutes later.

Ari stroked her face, silently noting the dark circles under her eyes. "You look exhausted."

"I'm fine."

Sage stepped off the elevator and rushed over to where they were sitting. "How is Joshua?" She sounded breathless, as if she had been running. "I tried to get here as fast as I could."

"He's in the pediatric ICU," Ari announced. "They are giving him antibiotics to kill the infection."

"Let's pray," his sister suggested. "Let's do it right now."

Sage took Natasha's hand in her right hand and Ari's in her left. She closed her eyes and began to pray.

When she was done, she gave Natasha a hug. "He's going to be fine — I can feel it."

Ari left them alone to talk. He walked over to a nearby window and stared out.

Being in a hospital evoked so many memories of April and her suffering.

"You're thinking about April, aren't you?"

He turned around to face his sister. "Yeah, I was. I hate hospitals because they remind me of death."

"There's also life around us. Just think . . .

there are beautiful little babies being born as we speak. There are lives being saved right here in this hospital, like little Joshua's. This is where he will get the help he needs, Ari."

Tears formed in his eyes. "I can't lose him, too."

"You won't," Sage promised. She wrapped her arms around him. "I can't tell you how I know this, but I do. Joshua will be fine."

Ari and Sage walked back over to where Natasha was sitting.

"Honey, why don't you go home and get some sleep," Ari suggested. "I will stay here with Joshua."

"I can't leave him."

"I will be right here," he promised. "You look like you're about to pass out from exhaustion."

"C'mon," Sage said. "I'll drive you home and stay there while you get some sleep. Ari will call if you're needed at the hospital."

"I'll only be gone for a couple of hours," Natasha told him.

"I'll be right here."

Natasha didn't look as if she wanted to leave.

Blaze arrived and asked, "What can I do to help?"

"Maybe you can convince Natasha to go

home and get some rest," Ari responded.

"I have a better suggestion," Blaze said. "Check her into the hotel across the street. Sage, you go to her place and pack a bag for Natasha. Ari and I will stay here with Joshua. If the hospital needs you for anything, you will only be across the street."

Ari nodded in agreement.

"I like this idea much better," Natasha said. "I'm only going to be gone for two hours, though."

Sage took her by the hand. "Let's get you checked into the hotel."

"Don't worry, Ari. Sage will take care of Natasha," Blaze said.

"What are you doing here?"

Blaze smiled. "I came to make sure you're okay. It's hard being in a place like this and not think about April."

"I do think of April, but right now, I fear losing Joshua most. I feel like I'm on the verge of losing a child."

"You love the kid," Blaze murmured. "I don't know if you've realized it, but Joshua is a permanent part of your life — our lives. You and Natasha need to work through your issues, because you love each other deeply. I'm not diminishing the love you have for April, but what you feel for Natasha is just as strong."

"I do love Natasha. She is my friend and I can't see the rest of my life without her. I will always cherish my memories of my life with April, but I'm ready to start living again. Natasha gave me my life back."

"Big brother, I think you know what you have to do," Blaze stated.

Ari walked over to the nurse's station. "I'd like to see Joshua LeBlanc. I won't stay long. I just need to see him."

"You can go in for five minutes," she told him.

Ari's eyes filled with tears when he saw Joshua's tiny body attached to a monitor. There was another machine connected to his finger like a small bandage which emitted a soft red light.

It broke his heart to see Joshua's small frame with so many lines attached. He was being given several different medications intravenously.

Blaze was right. Ari knew what he had to do. He eased out of the room and returned to the waiting area.

"You okay?" Blaze inquired.

"I need you to do me a favor," Ari told him.

They walked over near the window so that he could tell Blaze his plan.

His brother grinned. "I'll take care of everything."

CHAPTER 24

Natasha felt a little better after her shower. She was still tired from her nap, but she hadn't slept well because she couldn't stop thinking about Joshua. She sat on the bed with a towel wrapped around her.

There was a soft knock on the door, and then she heard the lock turn.

Sage stuck her head inside. "It's just me." She strolled inside with an overnight bag for Natasha.

"Thanks for packing a bag for me," Natasha said. "And for staying with me."

"We're friends."

She pulled out a pair of black jeans, a purple-and-black graphic T-shirt and under-garments. "I'll be back in a few."

Natasha padded barefoot into the bathroom to get dressed.

She came out a few minutes later, running her fingers through her hair. Natasha noticed a shopping bag on the bed.

"What's that?"

"It's the new video game Joshua wanted," Sage said. "Ari called me and asked me to pick it up. He wants Joshua to see it when he wakes up."

"Your brother is a sweetheart."

"If you say so," Sage responded with a chuckle.

"I don't know if I could've made it without him today. He is such a good man, but I really messed things up."

"Ari still loves you, Natasha. But I'd like to know if you love him. Do you love my brother as much as he loves you?"

She met Sage's gray-eyed gaze. "I love him with everything that I am. I never played with his feelings."

"I believe you, Natasha. However, Ari is the one you have to convince. He's been through a devastating loss. I don't want him to have to suffer heartbreak a second time."

Natasha ran her fingers through her hair. "Can we go back to the hospital, please?"

"Did you get any rest?"

"I slept for about forty-five minutes," Natasha said. "I just want to be near my baby."

Sage sighed softly. "Ari's going to kill me, but let's go."

They went back to the hospital.

"Did you get some sleep?" Ari asked when

they showed up in the waiting area.

"I slept for forty-five minutes," she told him. "All I could think about was getting back here to Joshua."

The doctor came out and announced, "Joshua is awake and he's asking for you."

"Thank you," Ari whispered, lifting his eyes heavenward.

"He's awake," Natasha repeated, tears in her eyes. "Joshua is awake."

"Go see him," Ari told her. "We'll be right here when you get back."

He could feel the heat of his sister's eyes on him. "What is it, Sage?"

"I'm convinced that Natasha really loves you, Ari. She wasn't running a game on you. You would be a fool not to take her back."

"Ari has this under control," Blaze told Sage.

She looked at Ari and asked, "What's he talking about?"

"Natasha and I have to sit down and talk when Joshua is out of danger. There are some things we need to discuss. Grownup stuff, so don't bother asking."

"Ha-ha, you are so funny," she uttered. "But I'm happy to hear that you two will be having a long-overdue conversation."

Ari wrapped his arms around Natasha when she returned to the waiting area. "I told you that he would be fine."

"Thank you so much for being here with me. I don't know if I could've made it without you."

They shared a kiss.

"I'm going to stay here at the hospital tonight with Joshua," Ari said, slowly releasing her. "I want you to go back over to the hotel and get a good night's sleep."

"Ari, I'm fine," she argued. "I can stay here."

He shook his head. "We're not going to fuss and fight about this."

"I have an idea," Blaze interjected. "Why don't you both go over to the hotel? You can have a nice dinner, and then you both can get some sleep. I will stay here with Joshua."

"I'll stay here with Blaze," Sage offered. "We'll be here until you two return tomorrow morning."

Natasha glanced over at Ari, who asked, "What do you think?"

"You'll call me if Joshua needs me?" she questioned.

"Of course," Sage answered. "Remember, you'll only be across the street. Blaze and I can handle things on this end."

"You were quiet during dinner," Ari commented when they returned to the hotel room. "Are you still worried about Joshua?" He had finally gotten Natasha to eat something.

"I'm just sitting here amazed," she responded. "So much has happened between us, yet you never once hesitated to be here for me and Joshua. My ex-husband couldn't stay around to meet his own son."

"Some men are not meant to be fathers."

"Calvin clearly wasn't," Natasha responded. "Ari, I am so sorry about everything."

"Honey, you don't have to keep apologizing. If it had been me, I would have done anything for my son. I had no right to pass judgment on you like that."

She gazed up at him. "I love you so much."

The touch of his lips on hers was a delicious sensation. Natasha had missed his kisses.

"I missed holding you like this," Ari whispered. He bent his head, kissing her neck.

Natasha returned his kisses with reckless abandon.

Ari stepped away from her as if he were about to speak, but he couldn't take his eyes off her. He just stood there looking at the woman he loved.

Natasha breathed lightly between parted lips. She didn't say a word, but he could see her desire in her gaze.

He helped her undress.

Ari removed his clothes then picked her up and carried her over to the bed. His gentle massage sent currents of desire through Natasha.

When he was done, he pulled her close to him.

No words were spoken from their lips; they communicated only through their hearts and their passion.

Ari and Natasha were back at the hospital early the next morning.

Shortly after seven, the doctor informed them that Joshua would be moved into a private room.

"Who arranged for a private room?" Natasha asked.

"I did," Ari replied. "I also asked that they put a bed in there for you."

Natasha smiled. "Thank you."

"Mom and Dad are here," Sage announced.

Natasha felt a wave of apprehension as she walked up to them. "Thank you both for coming."

"We wanted to see if there was anything

we could do for your son," Barbara said. "Blaze called and told us he was being moved out of ICU this morning. I hope you don't mind that he's been giving us updates."

"I don't mind you and Mr. Alexander knowing about Joshua's condition," Natasha assured her. "I really appreciate your concern." She paused a heartbeat before saying, "I'm truly sorry for my part in Harold's attempt to take the company away from you."

Malcolm placed a reassuring arm around her. "You didn't really do any harm, Natasha. I have good instincts when it comes to people, and I knew you wouldn't let me down. When I heard what you did with the cashier's check Harold sent — it was confirmation. You are a smart young lady and you've made quite a name for yourself in this industry. Closing your business would be a shame. To that end, I have something for you." He handed her an envelope.

Natasha stared at the certified check for one million dollars. When she found her voice, she said, "I — I can't accept this." She met Malcolm's steady gaze. "I don't deserve your help after what I did to you."

Ari placed a hand on her shoulder. "He's doing this to keep you honest."

She surprised them all when she suddenly burst into tears.

He pulled her into his arms. "Natasha, I'm sorry. It was supposed to be a joke."

She wiped her face with the back of her hands. "I just feel badly about everything."

"You don't have to," Barbara responded as she handed Natasha a tissue. "Dear, we understand why you agreed to help Harold DePaul. You were close to his uncle, and then he paraded all that money in front of you. If I had been in your position, I would have done whatever I had to do to take care of my children."

"The money is yours, Natasha," Malcolm stated. "No strings attached."

She embraced Malcolm and then Barbara.

"We're going to check on Joshua," Ari announced as he took Natasha by the hand.

Inside the room, Joshua lay sleeping in the bed.

Ari turned Natasha so that she faced him. "I was going to wait until Joshua was home, but I can't."

"What is it?" she asked.

"I love you, Natasha. I love Joshua as if he were my own son. I never thought I'd get married again, but I can't see my life without the two of you in it. What I feel for you came out of nowhere, but it's made me realize just how lonely I felt. I don't want to lose you, sweetheart."

"I love you, Ari," Natasha responded. "But I know that we have a lot to work through. I have to regain your trust."

"I understand your reasons for working with Harold. I am not going to hold this over your head, because when it comes to family we will do whatever is necessary to keep them safe." Ari reached into his pocket and pulled out a tiny black velvet box. "I've had this for a couple of weeks now. I was waiting for the right time, and it's now."

He opened the box to reveal a two-carat, round engagement ring. "Natasha, will you marry me?"

"Say yes, Mommy," Joshua said, opening his eyes.

"You're awake," Natasha exclaimed. She rushed over to the bed. "Honey, I'm so happy to see those gorgeous eyes of yours."

"Boys don't have gorgeous eyes," he grumbled.

Joshua tried to sit up in bed, but Natasha shook her head. "Just lay there, baby."

He gestured for Ari to join them.

"I want Ari to be my daddy. Can he edopt me?"

Natasha glanced over at Ari and laughed. "It's adopt, sweetie, but we have to ask Ari how he feels about it. It's a really big decision."

Joshua looked in Ari's direction. "Will you please edopt . . . aydopt me? All the kids in my class have daddies but me."

"I would love to be your father," Ari responded, his voice breaking. "In fact, I'd like to get the paperwork started as soon as possible."

Natasha met his gaze with a smile. "I want that, also. Ari, I would be honored to be your wife."

Joshua reached out and took Ari by the hand. "Do I have to wait until the wedding to start calling you Daddy?"

Ari shook his head. "You can call me Daddy anytime, son."

"I love you," Joshua whispered.

"I love you, too." Ari sat down on the side of the bed. "Now I would like for you to get some rest. Your mother and I want you to get well, so that we can take you home. We have a wedding to plan."

"Nothing too fancy," she responded. "Just family. We can even have a barbecue reception."

"You are definitely the woman for me," Ari said with a chuckle.

"Natasha and I have an announcement to make," Ari told his parents when they joined them in the hospital room. "We're engaged."

Barbara broke into a big smile. "This is the best news. I'm so happy for the three of you."

"Mr. Ari . . . I mean Daddy is gonna edopt . . . I mean aydopt me, so can I call you Grandmama?" Joshua asked.

"You sure can," she told the little boy. "And now that we have that straight, I'm going to sit right here and read you a story. Would you like that?"

"How about I read the story to you?" he countered. "I love to read."

Barbara kissed Joshua on the forehead. "We are going to have so much fun when we get you out of this hospital."

Malcolm walked over to the bed. "Hey, young man, what are you going to call me?"

Joshua thought about it for a moment, and then said, "I already have a Nana and a Pop, so I think I'ma call you Grandpa."

"That's a mighty fine name and I'll answer to it proudly," Malcolm responded with a smile.

"My parents are on their way from the airport," Natasha announced. "I just received a text from them. They're going to be relieved to see Joshua and how well he's doing."

Ari wrapped an arm around her. "When

do you want to tell them our news?"

"If we don't tell them right away, I'm sure Joshua will," Natasha responded. "He's so excited about having you as a father."

"What about you? Are you excited about having me as a husband?"

She pulled his face to hers, kissing him passionately. "I can't wait to be your wife."

"Not in front of the child," Blaze uttered.

They brought Joshua home from the hospital two days later.

Natasha's parents were in the kitchen preparing dinner for them. Her brother and his family were due to arrive at any moment, and her sister would be flying in tomorrow morning.

"Let's get you settled down in here," Ari said, as he helped the little boy into his bed.

"I'm so glad to be out of that hospital."

"I bet you are," Natasha said. "I know I'm thrilled to have you home with me."

Joshua looked up at Ari and asked, "Dad, can you stay in here with me until I fall asleep?"

He never tired of hearing Joshua call him that. "Sure."

"Hey, what about me?" Natasha asked. "I can't hang out in here with you and Ari?"

"Mama, it's just boys right now," Joshua

explained. "You can help Nana and Pop in the kitchen."

"Oh, okay," she murmured. "If you really want me to leave."

"Just for a little while. I want to talk to Dad man-to-man."

Ari winked at her.

"Have fun," she said before closing the door.

"Dad, there's something I really want to tell you," Joshua began.

"What is it?"

"I don't know why my real dad never wanted me, but it doesn't hurt so much since I met you."

Ari blinked back tears. "What happened with your father is his fault — not yours. One day he's going to regret missing out on such a wonderful son."

Joshua grinned. "I'm sure glad I got to pick you as my dad."

"Me, too."

He stayed with Joshua until he fell asleep.

"He's sleeping," Ari announced when he entered the kitchen.

"He's still so weak," Natasha responded. "But I'm glad he's home. He always seems to do much better when he is in his own room."

"Joshua is going to be fine," Corrine

stated as she patted Ari on the arm. "Thanks to the generosity of your family, my grandson will have the best medical care that money can buy."

"Mama's right," Natasha interjected. "I will never forget what your parents did for Joshua."

"They are good people, Natasha, and they love children," Ari responded. "Besides, we are going to be a family. Oh, we are all going to test for bone-marrow donation."

Tears filled her eyes. "Really?"

Ari nodded. "I love you, Natasha. I love Joshua and I am not going to stop fighting this disease."

"Ari, I fell in love with you the moment I met you."

He gave her a surprised look. "Really? I was under the impression that you didn't like me."

Natasha shook her head. "Oh, no, I was very attracted to you, but I thought you were married. Even after I found out you were a widower, I didn't want to admit to myself how much I cared about you."

"Why? Because you saw me as the enemy?"

She smiled. "Yeah, something like that. I greatly admired Robert DePaul, and I felt like the hotels should have stayed with the family. When Harold came to me, I accepted his offer, but I had no idea what he was doing. I never thought he'd do something so underhanded with the contractors. But then he wanted me to go against my moral beliefs, and I couldn't do that — that's when things became contentious between us."

"Natasha, I understand your loyalty to the DePaul family. In some way, I respect it."

"My loyalty belongs to you and your family."

Ari pulled her into his arms, kissing her.

"I never thought I'd ever love again, but out of nowhere, you breezed into my life and gave me a reason to live again. To love and be loved — it really is the greatest gift of all."

ABOUT THE AUTHOR

Jacquelin Thomas is an award-winning, bestselling author with more than thirty-five books in print. When she is not writing, she is busy working toward a degree in psychology. Jacquelin and her family live in North Carolina.